D0097794

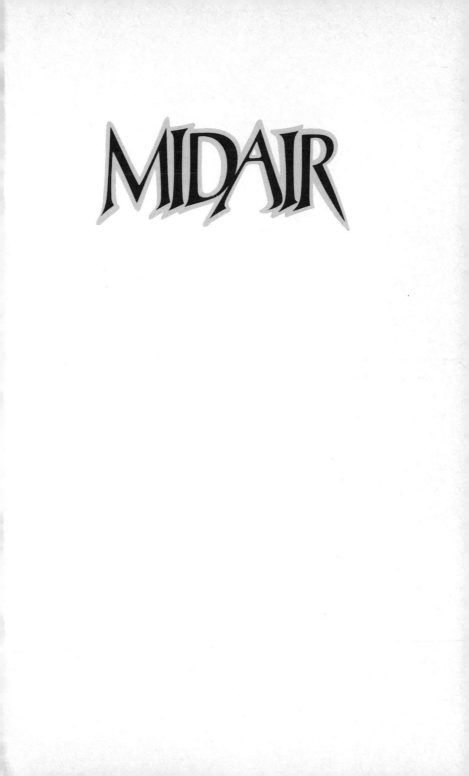

MIDAIR

Books by Frank Conroy

STOP–TIME

MIDAIR

MIDAIR

E. P. DUTTON · SEYMOUR LAWRENCE / NEW YORK

FRANK CONROY

The following stories originally appeared in *The New Yorker:*

"Car Games" (January, 1970)
"The Mysterious Case of R" (August, 1970)
"Celestial Events" (June, 1974)
"Midair" (February, 1984)

The story "Roses" originally appeared in *Ararat,* Winter 1975.

Published in the United States by
E. P. Dutton, a division of New American Library,
2 Park Avenue, New York, N.Y. 10016

Library of Congress Cataloging in Publication Data

Conroy, Frank.
Midair.
Contents: Midair—Celestial events—Car games—[etc.]
I. Title.
PS3553.O5196M5   1985   813'.54   85-10154

ISBN: 0-525-24319-4

Published simultaneously in Canada by
Clarke, Irwin & Company Limited, Toronto and Vancouver

DESIGNED BY MARK O'CONNOR

10 9 8 7 6 5 4 3 2 1

First Edition

For Maggie

CONTENTS

MIDAIR

A sunny, windy day on the lower East Side of New York. The year is 1942. Sean, aged six, is being more or less pulled along the sidewalk by his father, who has shown up from nowhere to take him home from school. Sean tries to keep the pace, although he does not remember the last time he has seen this big, exuberant man, nor is he altogether sure that he trusts him. Mary, on the other side, is nine. Her legs are longer, and she seems happy, skipping every now and then, shouting into the wind, calling him Daddy. Sean cannot hear what they're saying except in fragments—the wind tears at the words. His hand, wrist, and part of his forearm are enclosed in his

3

father's fist. The big man strides along, red-faced, chin jutting forward proudly, his whole carriage suggesting the eagerness and confidence of a soldier marching forward to receive some important, hard-won medal.

He is not a soldier, as Sean's mother has recently explained. He is not in the Army (although a war is going on) but in something called a rest home, where people go in order to rest. He does not seem tired, Sean thinks.

"It'll be a different story now, by God," his father says as they turn the corner onto Seventh Street. "A completely different story." Energy seems to radiate from the man like an electrical charge. His body carries a pale-blue corona, and when he speaks his white teeth give off white lightning. "What a day!" He lets go of the children's hands and makes a sweeping gesture. "An absolute pip of a day. Look at that blue sky! The clouds! Seventh Street! Look how vivid the colors are!"

Sean cannot look. He is preoccupied with the unnatural force of his father's enthusiasm. It is as if all that has been pointed out is too far away to be seen. The boy's awareness is focussed on the small bubble of space immediately surrounding himself, his father, and his sister. Within that area he sees clearly—as if his life depended on it—and there is no part of him left over to see anything else.

They reach the tenement building and climb the stoop. His father hesitates at the door.

"The key," he says.

"Mother has it," Mary says.

"You haven't got it?" He rolls his head in exasperation.

"I'm sorry." Mary is afraid she has failed him. "I'm sorry, Daddy."

Sean is uneasy with her use of the word "Daddy." It sounds strange, since they never use it. It is not part of their domestic vocabulary. On those extremely rare occasions when Sean, Mary, and their mother ever mention the man, the word they have always used is "Father."

Mrs. Rosenblum, second floor rear, emerges from the house.

"Good morning," his father says, smiling, catching the door. "In you go, children."

Mrs. Rosenblum has never seen this big man before but recognizes, from his expensive clothes and confident manner, that he is a gentleman, and the father of the children. A quick glance at Mary, smiling as he touches her head, confirms everything.

"Nice," Mrs. Rosenblum says. "Very nice."

Inside, Sean's father takes the steps two at a time. The children follow up to the top floor—the fourth—and find him standing at the door to the apartment, trying the knob.

"No key here, either, I suppose."

"It's the same one," Mary says.

He gives the door a hard push, as if testing. Then he steps back, looks around, and notices the iron ladder leading up to the hatch and the roof.

"Aha! More than one way to skin a cat." He strides over to the ladder and begins to climb. "Follow me, buckos. Up the mainmast!"

"Daddy, what are you doing?" Mary cries.

"We'll use the fire escape." He pushes up the hatch and sunlight pours down. "Come on. It's fun!"

Sean can hear the wind whistling up there as his father climbs through. Mary hesitates an instant and then mounts the ladder. As she approaches the top, Sean follows her. He ascends into the sunshine and the wind.

The big man moves rapidly across the tarred roof to the rear of the building and the twin hoops of the fire-escape railing. He shouts back at the children, but his words are lost. He beckons, turns, and grabs the railings. His feet go over the edge and he begins to descend. Then he stops—his head and shoulders visible—and shouts again. Mary moves forward, the big man sinks out of sight, and Sean follows.

The boy steps to the edge and looks over. His father is ten feet below, on the fire-escape landing, red face up-turned.

"Come on!" The white teeth flash. "The window's open."

The wind whips Mary's skirt around her knees as she goes over. She has to stop and push the hair out of her eyes. When she reaches the landing below, Sean grabs the hoops. Five floors down, a sheet of newspaper flutters across the cement at the bottom of the airshaft. It seems no bigger than a page from a book. He climbs down. Pigeons rise from the airshaft and scatter. On the landing, he sees his father, already inside, lifting Mary through the kitchen window. He follows quickly on his own.

The kitchen, although entirely familiar in every detail, seems slightly odd in its totality. The abruptness of the entry —without the usual preparation of the other rooms—tinges the scene with unreality. Sean follows his father and sister through the kitchen, into the hall, and to the doorway of his mother's room. His father does not enter but simply stops and looks.

"Have you been here before?" Sean asks.

"Of course he has, silly," Mary says rapidly.

His father turns. "Don't you remember?"

"I don't think so," Sean says.

As they pass the main door to the apartment, toward the front of the hall, his father pauses to slip on the chain lock.

For more than an hour they have been rearranging the books on the living-room shelves, putting them in alphabetical order by author. Sean's father stops every now and then, with some favorite book, to do a dramatic reading. The readings become more and more dramatic. He leans down to the children to emphasize the dialogue, shouting in different voices, gesticulating with his free arm in the air, making faces. But then, abruptly, his mood changes.

"The windows are filthy," he says angrily, striding back and forth from one to another, peering at the glass. The books are forgotten now as he goes to the kitchen. Mary quickly pushes them over to the foot of the bookcase. Sean helps. While doing this, they look very quickly, almost furtively, into each other's eyes. It takes a fraction of a second, but Sean understands. He is aware that his father's unexplained abandonment of an activity in which he had appeared to be so deeply involved has frightened Mary. His own feelings are complex—he is gratified that she is scared, since in his opinion she should have been scared all along, while at the same time his own fear, because of hers, escalates a notch.

"What's going to happen?" Sean asks quietly.

"Nothing. It's O.K." She pretends not to be afraid.

"Get Mother." The sound of water running in the kitchen.

Mary considers this. "It's O.K. She'll come home from work the way she always does."

"That's a long time. That's too long."

The big man returns with a bucket and some rags. His face seems even more flushed. "We'll do it ourselves. Wait till you see the difference." He moves to the central window, and they are drawn in his wake. Sean recognizes a shift in the atmosphere: before, with the books, there was at least a pretense of the three of them doing something together —a game they might all enjoy—but now his father's attention has narrowed and intensified onto the question of the windows. He seems barely aware of the children.

He washes the panes with rapid, sweeping movements. Then he opens the lower frame, bends through, turns, and sits on the sill to do the outside. Sean can see his father's face, concentrated, frowning, eyes searching the glass for streaks.

Sean begins to move backward.

"No," Mary says quickly. "We have to stay."

The boy stops beside the rocking chair where his mother sits after dinner.

The big man reënters, and steps back to regard the results of his work. "Much better. Much, much better." He moves on to the next window. "Fresh water, Mary. Take the bucket."

Mary obeys, and goes back to the kitchen.

The big man stares down at the street. Sean stays by the rocking chair.

"You don't remember," the big man says. "Well, that's all right. Time is different for children. In any case, the past is behind us now. What counts is the future." He gives a short, barking laugh. "Another cliché rediscovered!

But that's the way it is. You have to penetrate the clichés, you have to live them out to find out how true they are. What a joke!"

Mary brings the bucket of water to his side. Suddenly he moves closer to the window. He has seen something on the street.

"God damn." He moves back rapidly. He turns and runs down the hall to the kitchen. Sean and Mary can see him closing and locking the rear windows. "Bastards!" he shouts.

Mary moves sideways to glance through the window to the street.

"What is it?" Sean asks.

"An ambulance." Her voice is beginning to quaver. "It must be that ambulance."

Now he comes back into the living room and paces. Then he rushes to the newly washed window, opens it, and tears the gauzy curtains from the rod and throws them aside. Sean can see Mary flinch as the curtains are torn. The big man moves from one window to the next, opening them and tearing away the curtains. Wind rushes through the room. Torn curtains rise from the floor and swirl about.

He gathers the children and sits down on the couch, his arms around their shoulders. Sean feels crushed and tries to adjust his position, but his father only tightens his grip. The big man is breathing fast, staring into the hall, at the door.

"Daddy," Mary says. "It hurts."

A slight release of pressure, but Sean is still held so tightly to the man's side he can barely move.

"Oh, the bastards," his father says. "The tricky bastards."

The buzzer sounds. Then, after a moment, a knock on the door. The big man's grip tightens.

Another knock. The sound of a key. Sean watches the door open a few inches until the chain pulls it short. He sees the glint of an eye.

"Mr. Kennedy? This is Dr. Silverman. Would you open the door, please?"

"Alone, are you, Doctor?" An almost lighthearted tone.

A moment's pause. "No. I have Bob and James here with me." A calm voice, reassuring to Sean. "Please let us in."

"The goon squad," his father says.

"Bob in particular is very concerned. And so am I."

"Bob is a Judas."

"Mr. Kennedy. Be reasonable. We've been through this before, after all."

"No, no." As if correcting a slow student. "This is different. I'm through with you people. I'm through with all of that. I've come home, I'm here with my children, and I'm going to stay."

A pause. "Yes. I can see the children."

"We've been having a fine time. We've been washing the windows, Doctor." An almost inaudible chuckle.

"Mr. Kennedy, I implore you to open the door. We simply must come in. We must discuss your plans."

"I'm not going to open the door. And neither are you. What we have here, Doctor, is a Mexican standoff. Do you get my meaning?"

"I'm very sorry to hear you say that." Another pause —longer this time. "Bob would like a word with you."

"Mr. Kennedy? This is Bob." A younger voice.

"I'm not coming back, Bob. Don't try any crap with me. I know why you're here."

"I'm worried about you. You're flying. You know that."

"Got the little white jacket, eh, Bob? The one with the funny sleeves?"

"Look, if you don't come back they'll assign me to Mr. Farnsworth. You wouldn't do that to me. Please."

"Cut the crap, Bob."

"Listen. I'm with you. You know that. I mean, how many times have we talked about your—"

A tremendous crash as the door is kicked in, the frame splintering where the chain has come away. Sean is aware that things are happening very fast now, and yet he can see it all with remarkable clarity. Wood chips drift lazily through the air. Three men rush through the door—two in white uniforms, one in ordinary clothes. He knows they are running toward the couch as fast as they can—their faces frozen masks of strain—but time itself seems to have slowed down.

Still clamped to his father's side, Sean feels himself rise up into the air. He sees his father's other hand make a grab for Mary, who is trying to escape. He gets hold of her hair, but she twists away with a yell. Sean feels betrayed that she has gotten away. She was the one calling him Daddy. The wind roars as the big man rushes to the window and climbs out on the sill.

"Stop where you are!" he shouts back at the men.

Sean cannot see, but he senses that the men have stopped. He can hear Mary crying, hear the wind, and hear the sound of his father's heart racing under the rough tweed of his jacket. He stares down at the street, at the cracks in the sidewalk. With the very limited motion available to his arms, he finds his father's belt and hangs on with both fists.

"You bastards," his father shouts. "What you don't realize is I can do anything. Anything!"

Something akin to sleepiness comes over Sean. As time passes he realizes—a message from a distant outpost—that he has soiled himself. Finally, they are pulled back in, with great speed and strength, and fall to the floor. His father screams as the men cover him.

In college, his father long dead, and all memory of his father's visit in 1942 completely buried, Sean looks for a wife. He is convinced that if he doesn't find someone before he graduates, he will have missed his chance for all time. The idea of living alone terrifies him, although he is not aware that it terrifies him. He lives as if he did not have a past, and so there is a great deal about himself of which he is not aware. He is entirely ignorant of his lack of awareness, and believes himself to be in full control of his existence. He zeroes in on a bright, rather guarded girl he meets in Humanities 301, and devotes himself to winning her hand. It is a long campaign, and the odds are against him—her family disapproves vehemently, for reasons that are never made clear, and she is more intelligent than Sean, and ambitious, in a way he is not, for power in some as yet unnamed career. She is older than he is. She is not afraid of living alone. Yet in the end his tenacity prevails. Graduate school provides no route for her ambition, she drifts for a bit, and finally capitulates over the telephone. Sean is exultant.

They are married by a judge in her parents' midtown

brownstone. Sean is six feet two inches tall, weighs a hundred and thirty-three pounds, and appears, with his Irish, slightly acned face, to be all of seventeen. (He is actually twenty-two.) His wife is struck by the irony of the fact that more than half of the relatives watching the event are divorced. Sean is impressed by the activity outside the window during the ceremony. The New York Foundling Hospital is being torn down—the wrecker's ball exploding walls even as the absurdly short judge drones on. For both of them—in a moment of lucidity whose importance they are too young to recognize—the ceremony is anticlimactic, and faintly ridiculous.

Four years pass, and nothing happens. They both have a small monthly income from trust funds. She dabbles in an occasional project or temporary job but always retreats in mysterious frustration to the safety of their apartment. He writes a book, but it contains nothing, since he knows very little about people, or himself. He remains a boy; the marriage that was to launch him into maturity serves instead to extend his boyhood. Husband and wife, they remain children. They live together in good will, oddly sealed off from one another, and from the world. He dreams of people jumping out of windows, holding hands, in eerie accord. He has no idea what the dreams mean, or where they come from. She confesses that she has never believed in romantic love. They are both frightened of the outside, but they respond differently. She feels that what is out there is too dangerous to fool with. He feels that, however dangerous, it is only out there that strength can be found. In some vague, inchoate way, he knows he needs strength.

Privately, without telling him, she decides to have children. Philip is born. John is born. Sean is exultant.

A summer night in 1966. Sean drives down from Harlem, where he has gotten drunk in a jazz club. The bouncer, an old acquaintance, has sold him an ounce of marijuana. Sean carries it in a sealed envelope in his back pocket. He turns off the Henry Hudson Parkway at Ninety-sixth Street, slips along Riverside Drive for a couple of blocks, turns, and pulls up in front of Judy's house. It's a strange little building —five floors with a turret up the side, a dormer window on her top-floor apartment, bits of crenellation and decoration, like some miniature castle. A Rapunzel house.

He had met her on the sidelines during a soccer game. Kneeling on the grass, he had turned his head to follow the fullback's kick, and found himself looking instead at the slender, blue-jeaned thigh of the girl standing next to him. Perhaps it was the suddenness, the abrupt nearness of the splendid curve of her backside, the images sinking into him before he had time to protect himself. The lust he felt was so pure it seemed, for all its power, magically innocent, and he got to his feet and began talking to her. (She was eventually to disappear into medical school, but never, as it turned out, from his memory.)

He stares up at the dark window. Behind the window is a room, and in the room a bed, in which for a year he has been making love to Judy. She is gone now, away for a month, driving around France in a *deux-chevaux* Citroën leased by him as a gift. The room is dark and empty, and yet he has to go in. He does not question the urge. He simply gets out of the car and approaches the building. Once he is in motion, a kind of heat suffuses him. He experiences something like tunnel vision.

Inside, he scans the mailboxes. A few letters are visible behind the grille in hers. He opens the door with his key and runs up the stairs—turning at landings, climbing, turning, climbing, until he is there, at the top floor. It is midnight, and the building is silent. He slips the key into the lock, turns and pushes. The door will not open. He has forgotten the police lock, the iron bar she'd had installed before she left—with a separate locking mechanism. He doesn't have that key. He leans against the door for a moment, and the faint scent of the room inside reaches him. He is dizzy with the scent, and the door suddenly enrages him. The scent is inside, and he must get inside.

He pounds his shoulder against the glossy black wood in a steady rhythm, putting all his weight against it. The door shakes in its hinges, but he can feel the solidity of the iron bar in the center. There is not an iota of movement in the bar. He moves back in the hallway—halfway to the rear apartment—runs forward, raises his right leg, and kicks the central panel of the door. A terrific crash, but the door does not yield. He continues to run and kick, in a frenzy, until he starts falling down.

Out of breath, he sits on the stairs to the roof and looks at Judy's door. He cannot believe there is no way to get it open. The wood is cracked in several places. Finally, as his breathing slows, he gives up. The iron bar will never move.

Slowly, swirling like smoke, an idea emerges. He turns and looks up the stairs, into the darkness. After a moment he stands up, mounts the stairs, opens the hatch, and climbs out onto the roof. The air cools him—he is drenched with sweat. Purple sky. Stars. He crosses the flat part of the roof to the front of the building, where it suddenly drops off in a steep slope—a Rapunzel roof, tiled with overlapping slate. There is a masonry ridge, perhaps an inch high, at the bottom edge, fifteen feet down. He moves sideways until he comes to a place he estimates lies directly above the dormer window. He gets down on his belly and carefully slides his legs over onto the tiles, lowering more and more of himself onto the steep incline, testing to see if he can control his downward motion. Sufficient control seems possible, and, very slowly, he releases his grip on the roof and begins to slide. His face presses against the slate, and he can feel the sweat from his cheek on the slate. From somewhere off toward Amsterdam Avenue comes the sound of a siren.

He descends blindly and stops when his toes touch the ridge. Beyond the ridge, there is empty space and a clear drop to the sidewalk, but he is unafraid. He remains motionless for several moments, and his noisy brain falls still. He is no longer drunk. A profound calm prevails, a sense of peacefulness—as sweet, to him, as water to some traveller in the desert. Carefully, he slides down sideways until his entire body lies along the ridge. He raises his head and looks at the deserted street below—the pools of light under the street lamps, the tops of the parked cars, the square patterns of the cracks in the sidewalk—and there is a cleanness and orderliness to things. He becomes aware that there is a reality that lies behind the appearance of the world, a pure reality he has never sensed before, and the knowledge fills him with gratitude.

He moves his head farther out and looks for the dormer window. There it is. He had thought to hang on to the edge of the roof and swing himself down and into the window. In his mind, it had been a perfectly straightforward procedure. In his mind, he had known he could do anything—anything he was capable of imagining. But now, as he looks at the dormer window—too far away, full of tricky angles—he sees that the plan is impossible. He immediately discards the plan, as if he had been caught up in a story that ended abruptly. He no longer has any interest in getting into the apartment.

Moving slowly and carefully, as calm in his soul as the calmness in the great purple sky above him, he retreats. Using the friction of his arms and legs, of his damp palms and the sides of his shoes, he inches his way up the sloping roof. He reaches the top of the building.

Once inside, he closes the roof door behind him and descends rapidly. He passes the door to the apartment without a glance.

As his children are born, Sean begins to write a book about his past. At first he is ebullient, possessed by gaiety. He doesn't remember much—his childhood all jumbled, without chronology. There are only isolated scenes, places, sights and sounds, moods, in no apparent order. It seems a small thing to write down these floating memories, to play with them at a distance. It seems like fun.

His children, simply by coming into the world, have got him started. As the work gets difficult, the fact of his children sustains him in some roundabout fashion. His gaiety changes to a mood of taut attentiveness, as the past he had trivialized with his amnesia begins, with tantalizing slowness, to reveal itself. He knows hard work for the first time in his life, and he is grateful. Soon he finds himself in a kind of trance; after hours of writing he will look down at a page or two with a sense of awe, because the work is better than anything he could reasonably have expected of himself. He will live this way for four years. In his mind, his writing, his ability to write at all, is connected to his children.

He develops a habit of going into their room late at night. Blue light from the street lamp outside angles through the large windows to spill on the waxed wooden floor. Philip is three, sleeping on his side, his small hand holding a rubber frog. Sean crosses the room and looks at John, aged two. Behind delicate eyelids, his eyes move in a dream. Sean goes to a spot equidistant from both beds and sits down on the floor, his legs folded. He stares at the pale-blue bars of light on the floor and listens. He hears the children breathe. When they move, he hears them move. His mind clears. After half an hour he gets up, adjusts their blankets, and goes to bed.

At a small dinner party with his wife, in Manhattan, he becomes aware that the host and hostess are tense and abstracted. The hostess apologizes and explains that she should have cancelled the dinner. There had been a tragedy that afternoon. The young couple living directly above, on the eighth floor, had left a window open, and their baby girl had somehow pulled herself up and fallen through to her death.

"You're white as a ghost," his wife says as they leave the table. "Sean, you're trembling!"

They forgo coffee, with apologies, and go home immediately. Sean drives fast, parks by a hydrant, and runs up the stoop into the house.

"It's O.K., it's O.K.," his wife says.

He nods to the sitter in the living room and keeps on going, up the stairs, to the children's room. They are asleep, safe in their beds.

"We have to get guardrails," he says, going to the

windows, locking them. "Bars—those things—whatever they are."

"Yes. We will," his wife whispers. "O.K."

"All the windows. Front and back."

"Yes, yes. Don't wake them, now."

That night he must sleep in their room.

Sean lies full length in the oversize bathtub, hot water to his chin. When he comes home from work (he writes in a small office a mile away), he almost always takes a bath. Philip and John push the door open and rush, stark naked, to the tub. They're about to be put to bed, but they've escaped. Sean doesn't move. Philip's head and shoulders are visible, while John, shorter, shows only his head. Their faces are solemn. Sean stares into their clear, intelligent eyes—so near—and waits, showing no expression, so as to draw the moment out. The sight of them is a profound refreshment.

"Do it, Daddy," Philip says.

"Do what?"

"The noise. When you wash your face."

Sean rises to a sitting position. He washes his face, and then rinses by bending forward and lifting cupped handfuls of water. He simultaneously blows and moans into the handfuls of water, making a satisfying noise. The boys smile. The drama of Daddy-in-the-bath fascinates them. They can't get enough of it.

Sean reaches out and lifts first one and then the other over the edge and into the tub. His hands encompass their small chests, and he can feel the life in them. The boys laugh and splash about, slippery as pink seals fresh from the womb. They hang on his neck and slide over his chest.

His wife comes in and pulls them up, into towels. They go off to bed. Later, in the kitchen, she says, "I wish you wouldn't do that."

"What?"

"In the bath like that."

He is nonplussed. "Good heavens. Why not?"

"It could scare them."

"But they love it!"

"It's icky."

"Icky," he repeats. He goes to the refrigerator for some ice. He can feel the anger starting, his face beginning to flush. He makes a drink and goes into the living room. The anger mounts as he hears the sounds of her working in the kitchen, making dinner. Abruptly, he puts down his drink, goes into the hall, down the stairs, and out the front door. He spends the evening in a bar frequented by writers and returns home drunk at three in the morning.

A few years later, Sean drives home from the office. He has worked late, missed dinner. He thinks about his boys, and begins to weep. He pulls off the expressway and parks in the darkness by the docks. It occurs to him that he is in bad trouble. The weeping has come out of nowhere, to overwhelm him, like some exotic physical reflex, and it could as well have happened on the street or in a restaurant. There is more pressure in him than he can control, or even gauge, his pretenses to the contrary notwithstanding. As he calms down, he allows himself to face the fact that his wife has begun to prepare for the end: a whisper of discreet activity —ice-skating with a male friend on weekends, veiled references to an unknown future, a certain coyness around the house. When he goes, he will have to leave the children. He starts the car, and the boys are in his mind; he feels the weight of their souls in his mind.

He unlocks the front door of the house, hangs his coat in the closet, and climbs the stairs. Silence. A fire burns in the fireplace in the empty living room. The kitchen and dining room are empty. He moves along the landing and starts up the second flight of stairs.

"Daddy." Philip is out of sight in his bedroom, but his voice is clear, his tone direct, as if they'd been talking together, as if they were in the middle of a conversation.

"I'm coming." Sean wonders why the house is so quiet. His wife must be up in the attic. John must be asleep.

"Why were you crying?" Philip asks.

Sean stops at the top of the stairs. His first thought is not how the boy knows but if the knowledge has scared him. He goes into the room, and there is Philip, wide awake, kneeling at the foot of his bed, an expectant look on his face.

"Hi." Sean can see the boy is not alarmed. Curious, focussed, but not scared.

"Why?" the boy asks. He is six years old.

"Grownups cry sometimes, you know. It's O.K."

The boy takes it in, still waiting.

"I'm not sure," Sean says. "It's complicated. Probably a lot of things. But it's O.K. I feel better now."

"That's good."

Sean senses the boy's relief. He sits down on the floor. "How did you know I was crying?" He has never felt as close to another human being as he does at this moment. His tone is deliberately casual.

The boy starts to answer, his intelligent face eager, animated. Sean watches the clearly marked stages: First,

Philip draws a breath to begin speaking. He is confident. Second, he searches for language to frame what he knows, but, to his puzzlement, it isn't there. Third, he realizes he can't answer the question. He stares into the middle distance for several moments. Sean waits, but he has seen it all in the boy's face.

"I don't know," the boy says. "I just knew."

"I understand."

After a while the boy gives a sudden large yawn, and gets under the covers. Sean goes downstairs.

The time arrives when he must tell the boys he is going away. Philip is eight, and John almost seven. They go up into the attic playroom. Sean masks the storm in his heart and explains that no one in the family is at fault. He has no choice—he must leave, and not live in the house anymore. As he says this, the boys glance quickly at each other— almost furtively—and Sean feels a special sharp, mysterious pang.

Twelve years later, Sean stands on line at Gate 6 in Boston's Logan Airport, waiting to check in for Eastern's 7:45 A.M. flight to Philadelphia. He is gray-haired, a bit thick around the middle, wears reading glasses low on his nose, and walks, as he moves closer to the desk, with a slight limp, from a cartilage operation on his right knee. He wears a dark suit and a trenchcoat, and carries a soft canvas overnight bag hanging from his shoulder.

"Morning." The attendant is a black woman with whom he has checked in every Monday morning for the last two years. "It's nowhere near full," she says. "I'll upgrade you now." Sean commutes weekly between the two cities, and the airline has provided him with a special card. When first class is not full, he gets a first-class seat at no extra charge. She hands him his boarding pass, and he nods as he moves away.

He sits down and waits for the boarding call. Businessmen surround him, two military officers, three stewardesses, a student carrying a book bag from the university in Boston where Sean teaches. He doesn't recognize the student but watches him abstractedly. Philip and John are that age now. Sean recalls that when his boys entered college, in Washington and Chicago, he found himself easing up on his own students in Boston, softening his style despite himself.

The flight is called. He surrenders his ticket and moves down the enclosed walkway to the open door of the plane. The stewardess recognizes him and takes his coat. He settles down in seat 2-A and accepts a cup of coffee. The ritual is familiar and reassuring. Sean is at ease.

It had not always been thus. When he'd begun commuting, Sean was tense in the air. It had been difficult for him to look out the window without a flash of panic. In his fear, he was abnormally sensitive to the other passengers —controlling his anger at loud conversations, conscious of any intrusion, however minute, into the space allotted to him. Expansive people irritated him the most. He could not abide the way they threw their elbows about, or thoughtlessly stretched their legs, or clumsily bumped into his seat. He found himself hating the other passengers, cataloguing their faults like a miser counting money. But eventually, as he got used to flying, he began to recognize the oddness, the almost pathological oddness of his hatred, and it went away. Only on very rough flights did it recur.

Now he can gaze down through miles of empty space

without fear. He wonders why, and concludes that both his former fear of heights and his present lack of fear are inexplicable. The stewardess brings breakfast, and his right knee cracks painfully as he adjusts his position.

The tenth summer of Sunday softball. The game Sean helped to organize had become a tradition in the town of Siasconset. Philip and John began as small boys and grew to young men playing the infield. Sean's second wife had taken pictures from the start, and the effect was that of time-lapse photography—a collapsed history in which the father grew older, the sons grew taller and stronger, and everyone else stayed more or less the same. Sean stood on the mound with a one-run lead, runner at first, and two outs. The batter was Gino, a power hitter. Sean threw an inside pitch and watched Gino's hips come around, watched the bat come around, and heard the snap of solid contact. The ball disappeared in speed toward third base. Sean turned to see John frozen in the air, impossibly high off the ground, feet together, toes pointed down, his legs and torso perfectly aligned in a smooth curve, a continuous brushstroke, his long arm pointing straight up at full extension, and there, nestled deep in the pocket of his glove, the white ball. Sean gave a shout of joy, dimly aware of pain in his knee, shouting all the way down as he fell, twisting, utterly happy, numb with pleasure.

The stewardess clears away his breakfast. Below, New York City slips past. He finds the old neighborhood, even the street, but he can't make out the house where his first wife still lives. They have retained good relations, and talk on the phone every month or so. His second, younger wife approves of the first, and vice versa. Sean is absurdly proud of this.

"Do you ever dream about me?" he had once asked her on the phone. "I mean, do I ever appear in your dreams?"

Slightly taken aback, she had laughed nervously. "No. What an odd question."

"I only ask because you crop up in mine. What is it —eleven years now, twelve? You still show up now and then."

The plane lands smoothly at the Philadelphia airport. Looping his bag over his shoulder, Sean is out the door, through the building, and into a cab.

"Downtown. The Drexler Building."

In his late forties, to his amazement, and through a process he never completely understood, the board of the Drexler Foundation had asked him to direct that part of their organization which gave money to the arts. It is work he enjoys.

He pays the driver and stares up at the Drexler Building—seventy stories of glass reflecting the clouds, the sky. Pushing through the big revolving door, he crosses the lobby, quickening his step as he sees the express elevator ready to leave. He jumps through just as the doors close behind him, pushes the button for the sixty-fifth floor, and turns.

For a split second he is disoriented. Philip, his older son, stands before him on the other side of the elevator, facing front. Sean's heart lurches, and then he sees that it is a young man of Philip's age, size, and general appearance, delivering a large envelope to Glidden & Glidden, on sixty-four. For a moment the two ideas overlap—the idea of Philip and the idea of the young man—and in that moment time seems to slow down. It is as if Sean had seen his son across a supernatural barrier—as if he, Sean, were a ghost haunting the elevator, able to see the real body of his son but unable to be seen by him. An almost unbearable sadness comes over him. As he emerges from this illusion, he knows full well that his son is hundreds of miles away at college, and yet he finds within himself a pressure of love for the young man so great it is all he can do to remain silent. The elevator ascends, and Sean regains control of himself. Now he can see the young man clearly—alert, a little edgy, clear blue eyes, a bit of acne.

"I hate elevators," the young man says, his eyes fixed on the lights above the door indicating the floors.

"I'm not crazy about them, but it beats walking."

The elevator approaches sixty-four, but then the lights go out, the emergency light comes on, and it stops between sixty-three and sixty-four. A slight bump downward. Sean grabs the rail involuntarily. Under the flat white light of the emergency bulb, the young man is pale, gaunt-looking.

"Oh my God," he says.

They fall a few feet more.

The young man presses himself into a corner. His eyes are wild.

Sean is utterly calm.

"Oh God oh God oh God." The young man's voice begins to rise.

"This has happened to me several times," Sean lies. "In Chicago. Once in Baltimore. The elevators have brakes, non-electrical, separate from all the other systems, which automatically engage if the elevator exceeds a certain speed." This, he thinks, is the truth. "Do you understand what I'm saying?"

The young man's mouth is open, as if to scream. He looks in all directions, finally at Sean.

"It can't fall. It can't. Do you understand?"

"Yes." The young man swallows hard.

"We're perfectly safe."

Sean watches the young man as several minutes go by. He remains silent, remembering his own panic in airplanes, his own need for privacy on those occasions, guessing that the boy feels likewise. After another minute, however, he can see the fear rising again in the young man's face. Sean shrugs off his bag and crosses the space between them.

"Listen," he says quietly, "it's going to be O.K."

The young man is breathing fast. He stares at Sean without seeing him. Sean reaches out and takes the young man's head in his hands.

"I want you to listen to me, now. We are quite safe. Focus on me, now. I know we are safe, and if you focus on me *you* will know we are safe." The young man sees him now. He moves his head slightly in Sean's hands.

"Hypnotism," he whispers.

"No, for Christ's sake, it isn't hypnotism," Sean says. "We're going to stay like this until the lights come on. We're going to stay like this until the door opens, or they come get us, or whatever." Sean can feel the young man begin to calm down. He holds the boy's head gently and stares into his eyes. "Good. That's good."

After a while the lights come on, the elevator rises, and the doors open. The boy jumps out. "Come on, come on!" he cries.

Sean smiles. "This is sixty-four. I'm going to sixty-five."

The young man moves forward, but the door closes. The elevator goes up one floor, and Sean gets out.

That night, as he lies in bed waiting for sleep, Sean goes over the entire incident in his mind. He laughs aloud, remembering the young man's expression when he realized Sean was going to stay in the elevator.

Then he remembers the day in 1942 when his father showed up unexpectedly, took him home from school, washed the windows, and carried him out on the windowsill. He remembers looking down at the cracks in the sidewalk. Here, in the darkness, he can see the cracks in the sidewalk from more than forty years ago. He feels no fear—only a sense of astonishment.

CELESTIAL
EVENTS

L̲ewis stood by his mother's bed in the hospital. After a long illness her body had shrunk to childlike proportions. The special earphones he'd bought lay beside her head. He picked them up, coiled the wire, and placed them by the radio. She was supposed to turn up the music as her pain increased.

"Lew?"

"Right here."

"Did I get the shot yet?"

"About an hour ago."

Her stomach convulsed in a small spasm. "I lose track of time," she whispered.

The telephone woke him in the middle of the night. Naked in bed, he was told she'd fallen into a coma. He hung up and sat in the dark for several moments. An extraordinary alertness came over him. Faint sounds from the city streets seemed unusually pure, each sound separate from every other—all hanging in space like tangible objects.

He got up, dressed, drank some coffee, and took a cab to the hospital. The elevator man, who usually said something, was silent.

She lay on her side. He pulled a chair close to the bed and took her limp, extended hand. It was dry and warm.

"I'm here," he said, leaning forward. "That's my hand you feel." He sat very still, his face so close he could see the pores of her skin. He knew she could feel nothing, and yet he answered the slightest movement of her hand with a movement of his own. Patiently, he focussed himself— trying to slip part of himself across their hands and into her body.

Suddenly her eyes flicked open. He was impaled on their gaze. Her curled body straightened under the sheets with impossible speed, snapping like a carpenter's rule. Her mouth opened in a round O. An odd droning sound emerged from her throat, gathered force, and built smoothly to a scream. Recoiling, he fell over backward. When he raised himself from the floor, she was dead.

After the initial operation, in which her breast had been removed, he'd rented a car to take her back to the country. She was ready to go when he arrived at the hospital.

"I've been walking a bit every day." She went to the center of the room and raised her arm. "Bye-bye, girls!" The other women murmured from their beds. Two nurses entered with a wheelchair. Lewis picked up his mother's suitcase and the radio.

She moved around the wheelchair. "I don't need that." The nurses followed her.

"It's the rule," said the older nurse, taking her arm as the chair was wheeled into position.

"Just to the car, then." She lowered herself carefully, her thin body electric with eagerness. Lewis moved to take the handles. "Give me that stuff," she said. "I can take it on my lap."

He rolled her through the corridors, moving slowly. In the crowded lobby she gave him her Blue Cross card.

"Wow," she said.

"What is it?"

She looked around the room. "All this." She pointed through the glass doors to the street. "That."

The cashier behind the grille was as remote and efficient as a bank teller. When everything was done Lewis remained at the window, looking at the plastic card, and the receipt.

"Something wrong?" asked the cashier.

Lewis stared. Far back in his mind elusive thoughts floated, drifting like isolated candles appearing and disappearing in remote corners of a cathedral. How will she die? When will she die? What should I do?

After the long drive to her cottage in the country, they climbed the hill to the front door, taking it slowly. He kept his arm around her waist, and she was gay, as if they were dancing.

He prepared a simple supper, and when they'd eaten, and the dishes were done, he went down to the garage to look at her car. The wide door rumbled up into the shadows. A fine film of dust covered the white automobile. He got inside the car and switched on the interior light. Dust coated every surface. A spider's web hung inside the circle of the steering wheel. He started the engine, raced it for a moment, and turned it off.

As he walked back to the house, his mother turned on a light and he was startled by the sudden appearance of her face—an old woman's face—floating over a lamp.

She grew weaker through the winter. On a March night, just before dawn, he knew it was time. Listening through the wall, he heard her slow, laborious shuffling toward the bathroom. He called out, offering help. She answered— impatiently, angrily—and he suddenly realized she'd been sneaking, muting her gasps of pain for fear he'd discover how long it took her to get there. He resolved instantly to get her to a hospital.

At breakfast, he told her. Disappointment dimmed her eyes, and then fear brightened them. He spoke calmly, attentive to every nuance of her reaction. For a few moments she struggled in silence. He waited—saying nothing —and felt the precise moment of her acceptance with utter clarity.

He helped her get dressed, fetching things from the wardrobe and turning his back when it was necessary. Sitting on the edge of the bed in her blue suit, she held a pair of nylon panties.

"I can't bend," she said. "If you could just get them over my feet."

He knelt, hesitated, and then carefully slipped the panties over her ankles.

"You've taken plenty off, I'm sure," she said, a distant

smile on her face. "But how many have you put on . . . " Her voice trailed off. He turned away.

As they left the house she paused in the doorway to look back. For some time she stood quite still, as if she'd forgotten he was there. He was about to touch her elbow when she spoke—not to him but to the cottage itself. "Well," she said, "if I don't see you again, I won't see you again."

Walking down the hill, she held his shoulder and concentrated on each step. She spoke once, as, halfway to the garage, they stood resting. "Did you bring the earphones?" A slight sheen of sweat gleamed on her brow.

He drove toward the city on the old parkway—her favorite route—a gently winding road bordered by rolling swells of cropped lawn and stands of old trees. He discovered himself holding the steering wheel too hard. He'd take a deep breath and relax, only to find his hands clenched minutes later.

"You think I'll get out this time?" she asked suddenly.

"Of course." He lied in a casual tone. He seemed almost tranced on such occasions—unable to do wrong. "They missed something, that's all."

"Lew. One thing. No more radiation."

He glanced over despite himself.

"I want you to promise." She held his eye for a moment, and then turned away. "I couldn't take it again."

Later, he looked at her. She was asleep—head nodding to the movement of the car. Nerves twitched in her eyelids.

He drove carefully, maintaining a steady speed until a sense of apprehensiveness made him slow down and check the instrument panel. There was nothing wrong with the car. A faint tingling raised the hair on the back of his neck and hands.

Peering through the windshield he saw a change in the appearance of the world. Elusive transformations of some kind were going on wherever he looked—an eerie gleam on the surface of the road, colors going wrong in the trees, a peculiar dimness in the air. For a moment he thought he was going mad.

Then he remembered the date, and pulled over to the side of the road. She woke up as the car came to a halt. He rolled down his window. A deep stillness lay over the earth.

"The colors!" she said. "What's happening?"

"It's the eclipse of the sun. We forgot. It's today."

They sat in silence, watching the strange light. He wondered if she was frightened.

Her ashes remained in the funeral home for several weeks before he finally went to get them. In the large waiting room he sat beside a rubber plant and listened to footsteps on the marble floor.

"Here you are, sir." A small package, wrapped in brown paper and carefully tied with string. "There's an affidavit inside."

Lewis pushed through the glass doors and walked down the street with the package in his hand. It was smaller and heavier than he'd expected. In the car, he put it in the glove compartment, changed his mind, and took it out again. He drove to the country with the package beside him on the seat.

It was late afternoon when he arrived. He parked near the cottage and walked up the hill, past the house, toward the ridge, the package in one hand and a small trowel in the other. The air was crisp. Long bars of sunlight angled through the trees and leaves stirred around his feet. At the top of the ridge he went directly to a particular oak she'd once pointed out to him, sat down, and looked out over the valley. Miles away a highway was under construction—the bright orange earth-moving machines impossibly small against the raw dirt, like toys on a child's blanket.

He untied the string and removed the wrapped paper. He placed the small shiny can on the ground and sat watching it. His hands shook as he picked up the trowel. The blade turned on hidden stones, slowing the progress. Overcome by a sudden sense of urgency, he decided not to bury the can but to pour the contents into a thin, narrow opening in the dirt carved by the trowel.

He was afraid. Blood pounded in his head as he held the can, broke the seal, and twisted off the top to expose a muslin bag. He opened the drawstring and his fear vanished instantly. He saw a clean white powder with small, leached, porous bits of matter that had once been bone. He touched one of the lumps with his finger, poured the ashes into the ground, and covered them with dirt.

Walking back, he realized he still held the can. On an impulse he threw it high in the air, watching it gleam once, twice, and then again as it sailed through shafts of sunlight and disappeared behind the trees.

Workham the broker— pink, growing bald, and seventh on the club squash ladder—bounced back and forth, racket held precisely right, eyes fixed on the front wall. He was drenched with sweat, and as he turned, his pot belly formed a perfect dark circle under the clinging shirt. Lewis slammed the ball and Workham missed.

"10–9," Lewis said. He served and moved to mid-court. Workham dug into the corner and flicked a lob. Lewis volleyed, but Workham was in position, smashed the ball, and took the point.

"10–all," Workham said.

Lewis waited for the soft serve. A steady, conservative player, Workham invariably lobbed carefully placed shots to save his strength. Lewis met the ball in the air, Workham punched a good return, and a long rally ensued, each man fighting for control. They collided in center court, sweat flying from the impact.

"Let," Lewis said.

They began again. Lewis hit the ball harder and harder, recklessly stretching his body to the limit. A fierce heat possessed him. He took points without interruption and won the game.

"Rubber game," he said, holding out his hand for the ball. Workham moved slowly. "Ball!" Lewis snapped, banging his racket on the floor.

He slammed his serves relentlessly, forcing the game. Off balance, Workham could not effect his favored place shots, and both men ran full out, slamming and slicing, shoes squealing on the white floor. At 7–3 Workham sent a high floater to the back wall. Lewis barely managed a return. Secure in the T, Workham kept him running back and forth to the deep corners of the court. A balance was reached—Workham in the center stroking evenly, Lewis in back scrambling from wall to wall, unable to get any strength into his shots. He felt rage rising. His vision dimmed and points of light swam around him. As he ran for an alley shot, he realized the ball would be far enough away from the wall for a full swing. In the corner of his eye he saw Workham, facing away, crouched and motionless, his vulnerability at once ludicrous and infuriating. Lewis cocked his wrist and swung with every ounce of strength he could muster, trying to pour out his life, to explode his heart. The strings sang and the ball disappeared in speed. There was a sharp crack and Workham fell to the floor.

Lewis's mind went blank. He got up and walked around in a small circle, rubbing his back with his hand.

"O.K.?" Lewis asked. He felt dreamy. The court seemed to be stretching into a long corridor, carrying Workham away.

"Take the point," Workham said. He went to the receiving box and stood watching the front wall. Lewis was unable to move, but suddenly Workham turned away. "Take the match, for that matter," he said, with sudden anger. He left the court, slamming the door behind him.

Lewis put his back to the wall and sank to the floor, sucking great gulps of air. Sweat stung his eyes. He waited, and as his body grew calmer he imagined taking it apart, dismantling himself bit by bit, throwing a hand into a corner, sliding a leg across the floor, rolling his head like a bowling ball. He imagined himself in a dozen pieces, strewn over the white room.

Images from the hospital flashed in his mind, catching him off guard as he made coffee or took a shower. An old man shuffling down a corridor, bent over inside his chrome walker. The bright blur of rolling equipment—food trays, racks of X-rays, beds and carts sliding back and forth in the halls as if the entire hospital were slowly rotating in the air.

Standing with a doctor in the solarium, a large, bright room, empty save for a man in a neck brace watching a game show on television. I've told her the tests show nothing. Buzzers. Actually there are hot spots in both hips. Audience screams. The sound of an amplified clock.

Standing outside the door to her room one night while the nurse went in. A quick cry as the needle woke his mother—a thin, petulant wail of protest. An infant's whine, freezing his heart.

He bought himself new clothes, going from shop to shop in midtown. One afternoon, wandering through a large store, he felt dizzy. People rushed by, bells rang, elevator doors crashed, and he was forced to lean against a counter to steady himself. A display dummy stared through him. He pushed away and ran to a fire exit. A few flights down he regained control of himself. He sat on the cement stairs, his shoulder pressing the wall.

Walking home, he threaded through the crowds by reflex. Dazed, he lost track of time. He found himself standing in front of his apartment house, looking up at his own window. He shifted his weight from one foot to the other, back and forth, the shopping bags slapping against his legs.

An isolated sequence appeared and reappeared in his dreams, like a single strip of film randomly spliced into different movies. He would find himself floating in complete darkness, without weight. His hands would become visible, and then, gradually, the rest of his body. His brown suede shoes were significant for some reason he could not quite grasp. Lights flickered in the distance. Small points of light drifting toward him.

He kept the radio. He gave her clothing to charity, sent various personal effects to her friends, but he kept the radio. No larger than a book, encased in walnut with a dial down the spine, it stood on the table beside his bed. He listened without speakers, through earphones plugged directly into the tuner, as she had listened. He marked the good music stations and lay night after night in his silent room, hypnotized by the powerful effect of the earphones. Notes seemed to rise in his brain, welling up within as images rise in a dream. Melodies curved and fell away into unsuspected depths. He became aware of vast spaces within himself—long, open reaches where notes disappeared like lazy meteors.

He began to feel something behind the music, something hidden, unrelated to sound. A pressure drifting through harmonies. He felt a presence in sudden silences.

Lew. Listen. Listen. Lew.

Is it you?

Here I am. Here, Lew.

Suddenly afraid, he tore the earphones from his head. The room was dark. After a moment, he put them back on.

It's all right, Lew.

His mind became weightless. Thoughts swirled, floating, bursting into nothingness like champagne bubbles.

Yes. That's right. Yes. Do that.

A flood of tears poured from his eyes.

CAR
GAMES

The first time he'd ever driven a car entirely by himself was on his twelfth birthday. His uncle, owner of a Model A, had up until then allowed him to take the wheel for only a moment or two, retaining adult control of accelerator, brake, and gears, but on July 25, 1946, in a burst of largesse induced partly by the bourbon Uncle Charlie had already drunk and partly in anticipation of the bourbon they were on their way to the liquor store to pick up, the old man had gotten in on the right side and pushed the boy into the driver's seat.

"You mean I can drive?" Jack asked. The scope of the sudden, entirely unexpected present overwhelmed him.

"You know the gears," Uncle Charlie said. "Let the clutch out gradual and give it gas gradual."

"Wow."

Jack first looked at everything—pedals, shift, wheel and instruments—to make sure it was all still there. He rattled the shift, pushed the pedals, and began the moves he'd studied for years. The car jumped forward, lurched, and stalled.

"What did I do wrong?"

"I don't know. Let's go."

He started the engine, and the Model A took several large jumps forward. Jack was frozen at the wheel while Uncle Charlie dipped back and forth like a rodeo rider. Scared, Jack shouted at the windshield.

"What's wrong? What should I do?"

"Keep going. You'll get the feel of it."

In fear, when he meant to push the clutch, he pushed the accelerator, and after a moment of sheer terror the car moved smoothly up the hill toward the paved road into town.

"Good," said Uncle Charlie. "Try not to stall when you stop at the corner."

Jack was rapturously involved with the controls, adjusting the wheel, playing with the gear shift, experimenting with the gas. At the corner he simply turned to the left and accelerated.

"You should've stopped there," Uncle Charlie said, burping quietly as they shot down the hill.

"Wow," Jack said. "This is fantastic."

He remembers all this as he sits waiting for his wife to bring coffee into the living room. At the age of thirty-five he finds himself daydreaming constantly, remembering his past with such clarity it's like going to the movies. The previous afternoon, while on the phone half-listening to an important client, he'd gone back to the age of six, reliving a mysterious formal lunch in a country house where he'd asked for more strawberries, please. The client had undoubtedly thought he was making silent decisions. Neither does his wife know the extent of his daydreaming, putting it down to worry about the market, or perhaps, in her most fearful moments, to simple withdrawal after a hard marriage of sixteen years.

She pours herself a brandy. "You want one?" She'd started drinking when the youngest child had started school.

"I'm going to sell the car."

"You are?" She became alert—the special, slightly masked alertness she assumes when she discovers something has been going on inside his head without her knowing it. "To get a new one?"

"No. Just sell it. Cheaper to take cabs." He lets his obviously inadequate answer hang in the air, asking her to believe that after living as if there were no tomorrow for his entire life he has suddenly got sensible. The truth is he doesn't know why he no longer wants the car—anymore than he knows why he no longer wants to sleep with his wife. The car (a delicate, expensive, and unbearably beautiful Aston Martin) is no fun anymore. His passion (the sensation of being goosed when a gas pump was inserted into the rear of the Dodge, the lump in his throat, the ridiculous lump in his throat when he walked away from the Ford convertible for the last time) is gone, as if he had once possessed a separate automobile-loving heart that has atrophied and disappeared. His lack of feeling for the

Aston pains him. He wants to sell the car and become old.

"It's hard to imagine you without a car," she says. "You've always had one."

He drifts away, remembering sophomore year and the old Mercury he'd bought from Elvin Marsdale in French House. A big, top-heavy brute of a car, it had broken down constantly, forcing him to spend as much time in junkyards looking for parts as on the road. When, finally, his tuned ear told him the engine itself was dying—inexorable death from the inside, rings totally worn, valves gasping, drive-shaft groaning—he'd sold it to an ignorant graduate student at a slight profit.

For a while he had no car, and then an extraordinary piece of luck occurred—he won a Ford convertible in a lottery, a new model fully equipped with accessories, white walls, and a St. Christopher's medal. He suspected fraud, a telephone prank on the part of his classmates, but when he showed up at the rectory of an enormous church in down-town New Haven the car was indeed there, parked in an inner courtyard, and when he handed over the lottery ticket a fat priest gave him a set of keys, the registration, and a slap on the back. In the courtyard he walked around the car several times. The chrome gleamed with almost unbearable intensity. He could see a distorted image of himself in the waxed black body, his face slipping like oil over the curved surfaces. He was afraid to touch the car. When he got in he was afraid to start the engine. He stared at his eyes in the mirror (familiar blue—he was apparently there) for several moments before adjusting the glass. Then he pushed the seat back a couple of notches, turned the ignition, and rolled slowly out of the courtyard onto the street.

The car became his in time, of course, but it was never

entirely his. There was an aura of the supernatural clinging to it until the end, until trade-in. In dreams the fat priest asked for it back. He treated the car badly.

The first month or two he'd fussed over it, trying to keep it new, but as little scratches appeared here and there, as small electrical parts began to fail, as the smell of newness evaporated, he lost interest. He could not bring himself to clean the interior, and the floor gradually filled with newspapers, sweat socks, beer cans and Howard Johnson boxes. He began racing. A continuous night to night contest with Herb Maglio, owner of an old, but well tuned Plymouth. At first they simply raced from Starkey and Sheen's, the college bar, to the campus line—a distance of one mile, each man coming up with a slightly different formula every night. Eventually the race extended into the campus itself, along a difficult route they had tacitly agreed on—through the first parking lot, down the long curve to French House, a slalom through the trees bordering College Lane, up through the tennis courts and out over the grass to the cinder track around the football field.

Jack stares at his wife without seeing her and remembering the cinder track. Cold autumn air at three A.M. The lights of the cars were shut down for secrecy, and starlight, moonlight, points of window light from distant dorms needled the air. He stood beer-drunk with beer-drunk Herb at the edge of the grass and waited for his eyes to adjust to the dark. The smell of hot oil. A faint tang from swollen, burnt brake-linings. In the open car he gunned the engine, pumping gas like an organist pumping his bellows. Leaning back, half-standing in the seat, he threw a beer can into the night sky. When it hit the ground the engines roared and cinders flew. Wind swirled around his head. In the darkness the cinder track was absolutely black. An unearthly, perfect black. Follow the black.

He stands up abruptly, walks to the center of the room and looks around.

His wife watches him, and after a moment asks "What's wrong?"

He feels himself to be in some extraordinary state. The room around him is particularly vivid, each object clear and hard in space, the colors glowing, all of it entirely familiar, and yet he is no longer part of it, or, more precisely, at once part of it and not part of it. Simultaneously a sense of great power fills him. Profound changes occur in the dark parts of his brain, as if the lobes, like sliding blocks in a wooden puzzle, are gliding momentously into new positions and new alignments. He walks out of the room and out of the house.

At the entrance to the East Side Drive a dark blue Chrysler passes on the wrong side, cutting him off, and, rocking slightly, disappears up the ramp.

"Stupid bastard," he says as he negotiates the turn. "Goddamn bubblehead." He allows himself to rave at other drivers, insulting them as he never insults real people. He plays a game, spewing out a stream of oaths as he drives, ridiculing everyone on the road. He feels justified, since he knows he is a better driver than any of them.

He accelerates off the ramp onto the highway and catches a glimpse of the blue Chrysler crossing lanes on a curve up ahead. The Aston responds instantly as he presses the gas pedal half an inch closer to the floor. Sweeping through the slower traffic, he changes lanes smoothly and carefully. The speedometer needle rests at 70 and the engine purls.

One night after a light snowfall he and Maglio had taken their cars down to the new, unfinished parking lot behind the college Field House. At the brink of a gentle hill they stared down at a perfectly flat unbroken surface the size of two football fields, a smooth, unmarked coating of snow over the virgin asphalt.

"Beautiful!" he shouted across to the other car.

"You go first," Herb yelled back. "Bust the cherry."

Jack reached up and opened the roof clamps, pushing the steel front rib to free the pegs. With his other hand he pulled the switch and the power top folded into itself and disappeared behind the back seat. He turned up the collar of his jacket and started down the hill, timing his acceleration carefully so that the rear wheels maintained traction. He entered the lot on a straight line. Nearing the center he turned the wheel to the left and pressed the gas gently. The rear wheels broke loose, slipping to the right, and he steered into the skid. As the car stabilized, drifting perfectly over the snow at an angle of fifteen degrees, he repeated the same movements in reverse, swinging the car slowly through zero and over fifteen degrees in the other direction. Approaching the edge of the lot, he pressed the gas to the floor, spun the steering wheel hard and turned the car completely around in a four-wheel skid. For several moments he went backward, in a straight line, until the rear wheels collected enough traction to stop the car. His eye ran back along the elegant curves of his tracks in the snow to Herb's Plymouth, which was just starting down the incline. Jack slid out from under the wheel, raised himself up and sat on the back of the seat, staring through the snow-flecked air, listening to the faint rodeo yells of his skylarking friend.

After a mile he catches up with the Chrysler. The woman behind the wheel has black hair falling to her shoulders and her pale face is distorted. Alone in the car, she talks and gesticulates as if in the midst of a conversation. She drives abstractedly, the big car drifting back and forth across the wide road. Jack pulls the Aston into the lane beside her and she glances over quickly. She accelerates suddenly, viciously, but he is prepared, and keeps up with her. At eighty miles an hour they pass a string of cars, Jack on the outside, the woman on the inside. As the speed increases he feels a calmness come over his soul.

They'd played tag in the snow, spinning the cars around, slipping this way and that, Herb trying to touch bumpers, Jack trying to get away, their eyes blurred from the wind and the tears of their laughter. What times they'd had! What easy times, gliding, gently gliding over the snow like a pair of skaters.

As the road temporarily narrows to two lanes where some construction is going on she refuses to move over. He begins to pass but she moves closer to him and he is forced to touch the brakes. Side by side they enter the narrow part of the road. Before he can pull in behind her he has struck the rubber pylons, sending them high into the air, across the divider into the oncoming traffic. He is vaguely aware of workmen in the closed lane dropping their tools and starting for the barrier, but he is already past them. The light is beginning to fail as, on the other side of the city, the sun sets.

He pulls up beside her again, at ninety miles an hour. She is no longer talking to herself, but sits rigidly, staring straight ahead. She drifts into his lane but he does not give ground. The automobiles touch, side to side, with a soft sound like a tin can crushed underfoot. He pulls away for a moment, and then bumps her side again, somewhat harder than before. Pointlessly, mysteriously, she begins to blow the Chrysler's horn. When she decides to steer into him she starts the move so clumsily, so obviously, he is ready, and with a hard punch on his brakes he slows abruptly and she drifts into his lane, directly in front of him.

Ahead there is only a single clear lane. They enter at ninety miles an hour, the Aston two feet behind the Chrysler. Jack glances at the tachometer, shifts down into third, and closes the distance between the two cars. The slight jar as the bumpers touch is almost imperceptible. He feels a remote, far away pain from his clamped teeth. He presses the gas to the floor and listens to the Aston's big engine open up.

He pushes the Chrysler up to ninety-five, and then to a hundred before the first curve. She plows through a low iron railing and bounces high into the air. He follows her through the hole and for a split second they travel along the pedestrian walkway. Suddenly, as if a tire had blown, the Chrysler swerves, crashes through the high railing and sails out into the open air over the river.

That is the last image he sees—the big blue Chrysler suspended magically in the air above the black water, the woman inside comically prim, motionless as a mannequin. In another moment he would laugh, but the Aston strikes a concrete abutment and his head goes through the windshield.

THE
MYSTERIOUS
CASE OF R

D_{ear} Colleague,

Despite the obvious hazards of disclosure, I can no longer keep silent, as I have these many years, about the strange occurrences surrounding the case of R, one of my first patients when I took up practice in this country during the war. Those were lean years, as you doubtless recall, and I did not question R's assertion that he had picked my name at random from the *Journal of the American Psychoanalytic Association* in the public library. In fact I counted myself lucky, since he estimated his wealth as somewhere between twenty and twenty-five million dollars, and insisted, with the sort of idiosyncratic behavior toward money so common among the rich, on paying in cash at the end of each session. It was perhaps wrong of me to allow this arrangement. Nor did I examine closely enough my own slightly fugued state—a vague sense of well being—when, at ten minutes to four every weekday for almost three years a crisp one-hundred dollar bill was removed from an elegant ostrich leather billfold and placed on the corner of my desk. The regularity of the ritual was enormously reassuring—far more, indeed, than I allowed myself to realize at the time. At any rate (correction —at that rate) allow it I did, and subsequent events suggest that it made no difference to R, while at the same time it enabled me to take on B, the penniless Armenian composer with the shrinking genitals syndrome whose cure did so much to establish me in those circles in which I now move.

R was a particularly charming boy of twenty-seven, intelligent, articulate, and talented. He was the author, despite his youth, of two well-known novels (published under a pseudonym) remarkable for their poetic style and purity of conception. As an artist he strove for only the highest aesthetic accomplishment, never compromising, never losing sight of his goal, which was, in his own words, "the creation of an art which both contains and transcends life." He entered analysis as the result of an acute anxiety attack precipitated by six months of continuous drinking and indiscriminate drug usage. His history—orphaned at two, reared by professional nannies hired by the executor of his estate—in conjunction with his symptoms—recurrent anxiety, suicidal tendencies, somatization—and his first dreams indicated classical therapy, which commenced immediately.

He responded well. The more powerful of his self-destructive behavior cycles broke apart quickly, and as anxiety abated he moved into the familiar stage of object hunger, specifically focussed, in his case, on a desire to make love to beautiful women. But after a fast initial year analysis slowed down gradually, in exact parallel to a smaller and smaller output of prose from his pen, and in direct relation to his voracious sexual appetite, the size of which was one of the first clues as to the extent of childhood deprivation experienced by this sensitive boy. It was clear that a brilliant career lay before R, and I felt it my duty, not only to him but to society at large, to get him out of bed and at his desk. Further, since work provided the only extra-analytical continuity in his life which could possibly contain his energies, analysis could not end until a life style based on work had been firmly established. Therefore, in the third year, I began, very gently, to push him in that direction. To my complete surprise, and for the first time in his analysis, I met total resistance.

You are aware of the work I have done with artists. Three quarters of my patients have been artists. I have learned more about the relationship of the conscious to the subconscious, more about the dynamics of that quintessential mystery from my artists than from the literature of our own field. I have analyzed the leading poet, four of our best novelists, two painters, two composers besides the Armenian, a sculptor, and half a dozen actors. I am familiar with the special problems of creative people, and as you know from my published papers, I would be the last to insinuate myself into the mysteries of creation. Contrary to the opinions of some of our colleagues (most specifically that group over on the West side, what's-his-name's group) I assume that the reluctance of artist-analysands to delve too deeply into their work is entirely appropriate. The unconscious cannot be taken apart like a watch and spread out in so many shiny pieces on a table. The artists are correct—the source is unknown and will forever remain unknown. You can imagine, then, the extreme care with which I introduced the subject. R resisted every step of the way. After explaining that I was well aware of the dangers of any attempt to analyze the creative source, I suggested that he might not have been working because he was using all his energy in bed. He denied any connection, maintaining that he was not working because, at that moment in his life, there was nothing to work on. The girls were simply to pass the time until inspiration returned. He spoke of the Muse as an actual being, and diverted the rest of the hour into a lengthy free associative screen about certain rhapsodic sexual events recent in his life.

During subsequent weeks I became obsessed with R's case. I know now that it was all carefully planned. He was, I should be ashamed to admit, my favorite patient. Indeed, he still is. You cannot imagine how charming he was, or what a tonic it was for me that first year, to see him respond precisely the way patients are supposed to respond, making me the father he never had, his ego growing, strength and confidence building in him daily, guilt and anxiety draining away. Every analyst should have a patient like R once in his life. I was led into loving him, and as it turned out, that was the point.

On Tuesday, September the fourth, I used (for the last time in an analytic situation) the expression "writer's block," hoping it would lead to something. R laughed aloud, clapping his hands smartly in the air as was his wont when something amusing occurred (he was refreshingly at ease on the couch, having developed a whole set of gestures with which, although supine, he could express himself) and said there was no such thing as "writer's block." There were assuredly writers who, at certain times, could not write, but that was as it should be and was due to the intercedence of particular Gods whose special interest was the prevention of bad prose on earth. This seemed to me a significant fantasy, and I drew him out. To write without authentic inspiration, he said, was hubris, hubris in the original sense, a sin against the Gods. A somewhat confused dialogue followed, during which it gradually became clear to me that R was not speaking metaphorically. He meant every word. At the end of the hour he announced that he was an angel, rose from the couch, put a hundred dollar bill on the corner of the desk, and left.

I ask you, Doctor, to put yourself in my place. The rest of Tuesday and the beginning of Wednesday were a nightmare. I dealt with my other patients as if in a dream. How was it possible? After almost three years of analysis during which R showed not one schizoid symptom, not one single delusion, he seemed suddenly on the brink of disintegration. An angel! Had the ease with which we dealt with his neuroses been nothing more than an unimaginably elaborate schizophrenic ploy? Had I ever really known R?

I concealed my emotions during the Wednesday hour. Despite the danger of driving him deeper into his angel role I was determined to discover if it had been my insistence on discussing his work habits which got him there in the first place. Accordingly, he associated to his inability to start the next novel. He explained that he could not write because he was disharmoniously placed in relation to the Muse. I suggested that he might begin working nevertheless, in hopes that the Muse, and her favors, might somehow be attracted. At that point the following extraordinary events took place.

R announced that the Gods were pleased with my work with artists, whom they loved above all mortals, and that he, R, had been sent to dramatize the point, in the clearest possible terms, that I would otherwise have known only abstractly. It is right, he said, to help them collect their energies for art. It is right to clear away whatever stands between them and the full use of their talents. But it was wrong to suggest that they work in order to attract the Muse, not only because it displeases her to be called, but because such work tends to destroy the artists who create it. You must never forget, he said, and after this hour you never will, that the artist who works without inspiration creates a dead child, a child he nevertheless loves as he would a living one, and that the sensation of all one's work and love going into something not alive, as nothing can be alive without the Muse, is very much the same sensation you would feel if a patient you had worked your painstaking, dedicated work with for years, and come to love, were suddenly to raise his hand in the air, snap his fingers, and disappear. So saying, he raised his hand in the air, snapped his fingers, and disappeared. I remained motionless in my chair for some time. Eventually I got up and examined the couch, which was empty except for a crisp hundred dollar bill where his head had been.

I write this to you now, Doctor, without further comment. As you know, since my retirement, I have devoted myself to the study of Ancient Greek culture and religion. I grow old. I may be seeing R in the near future and I want to be able to say I had the courage to tell someone.

Yours,

HERMAN FRIMMLE, M.D.

ROSES

He woke at noon, and lay quite still, listening to hear if the girl was outside in the studio. Then he remembered she had left early, to go to work, and had touched his head on the way out. He had managed a sleepy word or two and she had laughed. He sat up. She'd been less afraid of the room—his bedroom, an enclosed structure in the middle of the studio, an environment for making love with bed, steps, and levels carpeted or furred—than most. She hadn't feared him either, and had retained the same voice, the same style of herself from Casey's Bar and Restaurant through the long walk home and into his bed. He got up.

He put water on the stove and ran, standing, in the cold air. One, two, one, two, knees up, knees up. When the kettle whistled he stopped, gasping for breath, flecks of light drifting across his vision. He drank two cups of black tea, took a shower, and got dressed.

Wandering up and down behind the work tables at the front of the studio he stared through the tall windows at the trucks unloading flowers downstairs. He lived in the wholesale flower district, surrounded by shops that were always full. The sidewalks were stacked with plants. In the summer their scent filled the air, in winter their violent colors burned in the gray light. Suddenly aware of the silence, the silence in which he lived most of his life and about which he was growing gradually more and more uneasy, he turned on the record player. The music brought back the mood of being with the girl.

At the work table he spread a large sheet of white paper over the wood and taped the corners down. He picked a hard Venus drawing pencil and began to work— work which was kind of play, as he laid down straight lines and improvised those curves and simple shapes suggested by the tensions inherent in the lines. He drew as little as possible, because each added element in any given problem geometrically increased the difficulties of solving that problem. Instead of building up an idea with more lines, he would, when he sensed an impasse, move to a new area on the paper and restate the idea in simpler form, or in a slightly different guise. His thoughts spread across the vast expanse of the sheet, appearing here and there like rocks exposed through the whiteness of a field of snow. He worked slowly, with total concentration, maintaining a special alertness toward whatever might reveal itself on the paper. After several hours, and several sheets, he stopped because he was hungry.

Inside Chu Wong's he sat at his regular table and ordered a beef chow. He was the only customer. The waiters sat around a large circular table in back working with their knives, preparing vegetables for the evening meal. He read the paper as he ate, fascinated by the news, not because he thought it was real, but because of the way it was prepared —a languid soap opera, an endless unfurling of large, meaningless events. At the end of the meal he read the social pages, looking for the names of those who had bought his paintings, amusing himself with fantasies about their lives.

On the street he threw the paper away, freeing himself not only of the paper, but of all that it signified. It occurred to him that the entire business of reading the paper in the first place might be in order to fully savor the moment of throwing it away, with the concomitant sensation of freedom and the reassuring feeling of time having been marked. He imagined an enormous metronome, a metronome the size of a mountain whose giant tongue swept slowly and majestically through miles of air to tick once, and only once, a day, at precisely the moment he dropped the newspaper into the trash.

Inside Herbie's Cut Flowers where the air was warm and thick with scent he searched his pockets for the slip of paper on which he'd written the girl's address. Herbie saw him from the back of the store and came forward quickly, his round face flushing, his hands already moving nervously as if clearing the way for the words he was about to deliver.

"Doctor Picasso!" Herbie said, falsely incredulous. "Again? Already? I can't believe it."

"Well," he said. "The deep rhythms of life."

"Yes," Herbie said. "What is it with you young people? Like rabbits. Unbelievable!" He took the slip, glanced at it, and looked up. "Is this a new one or an old one? I can't keep track."

"A new one."

"My God. The third this week and it's only Thursday."

"I thought you couldn't keep track."

"Don't give me a hard time," Herbie said, and reached for his order book. "What is it? Some drug? Some kind of pill? You look like a normal person." He copied the address carefully and returned the slip. "What should we send?"

"Roses. Two dozen if you have nice ones."

"I'll make believe I didn't hear. Morris!" When his assistant arrived Herbie tore out the page from the order book. "The big ones." Morris went to fill the order and Herbie pulled two roses from a bunch nearby. "Here. You deserve something."

He took the roses and moved to the door. Herbie rubbed a clear place in the steamed glass and looked outside.

"Was she nice?" Herbie asked.

"Yes."

"Fine. You're a young man. An artist. You should live."

"I'll see you," he said.

Herbie even opened the door for him, bowing slightly with mock deference.

He had not walked more than a few steps toward the studio when he saw a slim black girl coming in the opposite direction. He knew she was a model even before he noticed the elegant clothes and the large case she carried, the flat case in which models carry their photographs. As they passed each other, they looked at each other. Her brown eyes were steady. After a moment he glanced back over his shoulder, only to catch her doing the same thing. He took a few more steps and then suddenly turned around. She stopped and began to smile. They walked toward each other and met in front of the flower shop.

"The hardest part is already over," he said, and laughed.

"I guess so," she said.

Behind her he saw Herbie's face framed in the little oval he had cleared in the window.

"Would you like a cup of coffee?"

"Okay."

The florist's face was expressionless, floating in the glass.

She dropped her coat on the couch in the back of the studio and went to wander around in front while he made coffee. He put the two roses in a glass of water and brought everything out to the low table.

"It's ready," he called.

She came and sat beside him, laughing suddenly.

"What," he said.

"Nothing. Nothing. Me." She sipped her coffee and then looked at him. "I can tell you're straight. I could tell downstairs. I absolutely abhor freaks."

"So do I."

"This city is full of them. I'm from Chicago. I do magazine and TV work."

"I think I've seen you. The one with the Rolls Royce."

"Oh, that's old. I've done lots more. But it's nice, isn't it. I love that one. I make an awful lot of money. Do you?"

"I suppose so."

"What do you spend it on? Besides all this, I mean."

"I travel. I go away a couple of times a year."

"I work all the time," she said. "You have to jam it all in in a couple of years. I never get a chance to spend anything. I just mail it to the bank. I don't understand your paintings, by the way."

"That's okay," he said. "Don't worry about it."

"I'm not worried. I just thought I'd tell you." She pointed to the enclosure. "What's that?"

"The bedroom."

Through the enormous windows in the front of the studio he saw snow falling—the fat snowflakes of a heavy fall.

There was a reticence to her kisses, as if, although she had freely and on her own will removed her clothing and gotten into his bed, she had not yet committed herself. He held her in his arms and playfully chased her mouth. She turned her head, rolled over him, and jumped out of bed.

"Where are you going?"

"Don't worry," she laughed. "I'll be back." She did not leave the room, but went to the foot of the bed and struck a pose. "What do you think?"

He put his hands behind his head and looked at her. "Very close to perfect."

"Not too skinny?"

"Not for me."

"Some people say my behind sticks out."

"Do they really?"

"But my color is nice. Not too dark and not too light. You see the way it changes? What would you call it? How would you describe it?"

"Light brown."

"Light brown. What a thrill. My photographer says I'm a mixture of butter pecan and honey." She touched the screen of the TV set. "Very good for color. Is this color?"

"No. Come back."

She turned on the television and adjusted the volume so that there would be no sound. Then she came toward the bed. "You want me a lot, don't you? You're really desperate?"

He reached out for her. "You talk too much."

Her body moved constantly under his hands, shifting and turning with a slow rhythm as if she had given herself up to a dance. She moaned, and hissed as if in pain, and when he entered her she rolled her head from side to side, her entire body seized with a fit of trembling.

"Easy, easy," he whispered, moving gently, trying to calm her. But the trembling increased. Her hands moved mechanically up and down his back and her body started bucking as if in response to a series of violent electric shocks. He spoke to her but she didn't hear. Under closed lids her eyes rolled back into her head. She screamed suddenly, and he felt an icy splinter of fear.

Afterward they watched the small silent screen of the Sony.

"That's Betty Jarvis. The one in the Empire dress. She's sweet but she's on pills." She took a last puff of her cigarette and reached over him to put it out in the ash tray.

"Did you know that you scream?" he asked.

"Oh, I always yell. My African blood, I suppose.

73

There's Rina. She gets two hundred and thirty an hour now. Look at those ears." She sat up suddenly, her fists clenched in the air. "Look! It's me! There I am! Look! Look!"

He glanced at the screen—a shot of her face, her long body, flashes of sun, slow motion as she runs through a garden—and then turned back. Smiling, relaxed, she watched the screen.

"Oh God," she said. "It's so beautiful. So unbearably beautiful—and it's me."

When she had gone he sat on the couch staring at the two roses. Outside snow was falling and it was getting dark. Soon the phone would start ringing, as it did every evening, and his friends would tell him who was in town, where the parties were and where people were going. He would talk to all of them, collecting information, planning his night.

TRANSIT

Dear Colleague,

You have by now seen my report of the incidents of December twenty-ninth in the city of M——. Our superiors were aware of my presence in the city, so of course I had to write something. It has been circulated to all department heads, none of whom, save yourself, will bother to give it more than a glance. You taught me the art of writing official reports—the value of saying as little as possible, the absolute prohibition of personal observation—and you were a good teacher. Twenty-three years have passed, I am still here, and in line for the chairmanship. So the report is properly innocuous, but the reality was quite strange. I'm not at all sure I can describe it.

Something odd happened even before I got there. Standing at the window in the terminal, waiting to board flight 869, I noticed an ambulance beside the plane. A prone figure wrapped in blankets and strapped to a narrow stretcher was briefly visible in the rear of the vehicle as the white doors closed. Someone from the first part of the flight had fallen ill. (Flight 869 originates in Miami.) The ambulance drove away. I watched all this abstractedly, my mind elsewhere. The silence in which it took place, on the other side of the glass, gave the little episode a dreamlike quality. I saw it without seeing it, so to speak.

As boarding commenced, I made my way down the walkway, only to be stopped at the door of the plane by an attendant.

"You'll have to wait a moment, sir," he said quietly, as if not to embarrass me. "You have 3A. They're changing the cushion."

And so I stopped. The people behind me in the walkway stopped. The attendant gave a brief, apologetic smile. Over his shoulder, I could see into the pilot's cabin. Small lights glowed in the instrumentation—a density of dials, switches, and electronic displays covering every available surface—and the pilot (or co-pilot) sat motionless, his white collar tight against the flesh at the back of his neck.

Another attendant emerged from the main cabin carrying the bottom part of a seat, that part which we are told can be used as a flotation device in an emergency. It was heavily stained. I took the stain to be blood. He passed out of the plane quickly.

"Sorry for the inconvenience." The first attendant

waved me on. I wanted to ask what had happened, but there was a hushed mood in the air, a certain reticence in the attendant's eyes, and the question seemed, suddenly, indiscreet.

The flight lasted an hour and ten minutes. I was unable to concentrate sufficiently to get any work done, and spent most of the time looking out the window. At twenty-eight thousand feet it was still dusk, while below, night had fallen. Lights could be seen on the ground, separate, dim, wavering beneath a haze of purple smog.

It grew dark, and great cities slipped by underneath. The lights formed patterns, and the patterns seemed biological, as if one were watching clustering cells, pulsing arteries, and tenuous capillaries. I have learned to be suspicious of the grandiose ideas that sometimes come to me in airplanes, yet it seemed clear that we, the planners, the theoreticians of transport, should look to the biological model in our researches. Think of the efficiency of that apparent sprawl of systems the microscope reveals in the epidermis of a mouse! Elusive, half-formed ideas flitted through my mind, as if the scenes below were hinting at something, as if some great principle were about to be revealed.

We began our descent. The pilot had announced a snowstorm over the city of M——, and indeed, as we entered the clouds, the plane trembled. A series of sharp, abrupt jolts alternated with moments of smoothness. After fifteen or twenty minutes of increasing chop I recognized a germ of fear—enough to heighten my senses, so that I became aware of a change in the quality of the light. A paleness, no doubt because of the reflecting cloud pressing against the windows. But then we broke through the cover, into a light snowstorm, and landed without incident.

The generalized suspicion of bureaucrats prevailing in this country is probably healthy, but the image of us as faceless entities working without emotion in a sealed-off world has always puzzled me. How could anyone continue to work if the work meant nothing? If it did not connect? When I visit the airport at M—— I feel a sense of pleasure, a sense of accomplishment, still. Fifteen years ago we drew the master plan. Do you remember the complexity of the financing? The landfill question? The preposterous antics of the architect and his retinue? So many variables. I remember it better, no doubt, since it was my first large project. What elegance in that final three-hundred-page document! We had only to plug it into the system, like a piece of software, and everything happened exactly as planned. It was intoxicating.

And yet on this occasion I moved through the airport without really seeing it—as I had not really seen the ambulance behind the glass—filled with a vague sense that things were slightly askew. I could not shake off this dreamy, ominous mood.

The city fathers, in recognition of my help with the modernization of the transit system, had insisted on sending a car. However, it had been snowing a long time, and many of the roads were impassable. The car was not there, so I decided to take the subway.

The loop bus was jammed with travellers and baggage, but I managed to board, and we began the circuit. People were pressed together in silence, each individual maintaining his own bubble of privacy despite the crush. I noticed a tall man in a trenchcoat, with an overnight bag hanging from his shoulder, one hand grasping the chromium pole. He had remarkably wide-set eyes, which gave him a slightly amphibian appearance, and I imagined, as one does with interesting looking people, that I had seen him somewhere before. The driver's voice crackled through the PA announcing the airlines at each stop, and that was the only sound except for the shuffling of our feet as we adjusted our positions.

The airport transit station, as you no doubt recall, serves only those approaching it by bus or automobile at the far end of the airport loop. The station is elevated, and there is no entrance at ground level. We drove up the ramp, the doors sighed open, and everyone got out into the light snow and entered the station. A line formed for tokens, and it was some time before I stood at the steel booth, with its dark yellow shatterproof glass, and asked for a token through the speaker-phone. The man inside was an ancient Asiatic who did not look up during the transaction. His bald skull seemed fragile as an egg.

I pressed through the turnstile and joined the others for the long descent down the escalator. (It is the longest in the city.) In the fluorescent light the line of bodies, each one step lower than the one behind, glided along smoothly like a single entity, down and down into dimness at the bottom.

It was cold on the platform. I could see my own breath. The few benches available were quickly filled as people distributed themselves along the length of the concrete ribbon. Some stood with their backs against the wall, others sat on up-ended suitcases, or placed themselves directly under the lights, opening newspapers. I walked about two-thirds of the way along, put down my briefcase, and waited. Soon there was stillness. The people seemed like statues from the school of hyperrealism. I adjusted my scarf and turned up the collar of my coat.

As I waited, time escaped me. I remember being startled, as if from a trance, as a train, on the far track, going
in the wrong direction, roared out of the darkness and
passed through without stopping. I glanced at my watch and
was surprised to see that half an hour had passed. I moved
about a bit to get my circulation going. Fifteen minutes
later another train arrived on the far track, although this one
stopped. When it pulled out, a few uniformed airline per-
sonnel could be seen moving along, following the arrows
to the escalator.

After an hour, people began to move about restlessly,
some stamping their feet against the cold. I noticed a small
group of students, clustered around a pile of backpacks,
talking quietly. Two women a few yards away from me
began discussing possible explanations for the long wait, and
agreed that it must have been the snow. I knew that it could
not have been the snow. The entire system is underground.

At last a train arrived. The cars are of French manufac-
ture and modern design. The motorman's window is very
large—almost half the flat front surface of the car—and I
could discern the outlines of his body in the dark compartment, his head, his upper torso, and his arms extended down
and to the sides. He looked, somehow, like one of those
symbols from the international picture language one sees on
signs in airports and railroad stations. A triangular silhouette
meaning motorman. The train moved to the end of the
platform, and there was a great rush as everyone followed
it down. But the train did not stop. It slowed to a crawl,
accelerated, and disappeared into the tunnel.

Some people cursed. Others laughed, as if embarrassed
at having rushed down the platform to no end. Most simply

turned away, but as they resigned themselves to a longer wait, they all stayed together at the end of the platform.

Twice more, at long intervals, trains went through without stopping. Two more idiographic motormen, faces hidden in the darkness, two more tantalizing slowings, accelerations, and disappearances. Bewilderment and frustration in the crowd gave way to anger. Some beat on the sides of the train with their fists as it pulled away. A student went up to report the situation to the old token seller, but returned to say the booth was empty, and that the steel-mesh gates had been lowered, sealing off the station. A woman began to weep.

I was myself confused, as I struggled to come up with some explanation of these extraordinary events. Visualizing the system in my mind's eye, I tried to imagine what sort of computer malfunction might cause the trains to behave as they were behaving, but nothing ramified. And of course both the central and on-board computers are subject to motorman override in a collision scenario, and there was no such scenario in this instance. The more I thought about the matter, the more it seemed clear that what was happening was not possible. And yet, at some profound and nonrational level, it seemed inevitable, the culmination of that ominous sense of things being askew that had plagued me throughout the day. I had a very definite sense of having lived through the entire episode before.

We heard the faint rumble of an approaching train, felt the first slight stirring of the air. The amphibian looking man sat down on the edge of the platform, gave a little push with his hands, and jumped down onto the track, his overnight bag still hanging from his shoulder. He took his position, facing the dark tunnel from which the train would emerge, with a tight-lipped smile. The students started a cheer, and some of the rest joined in raggedly.

The train emerged, far down at the other end of the platform, and I could see (with relief) that it was decelerating. The amphibian man began to wave his arms over his head, and people at the edge of the platform did likewise.

Now the dark triangular shape of the motorman was visible behind the glass. Like the others, he was immobile, a cardboard cut-out. The train approached, slowing all the while, as had the others. The amphibian man held his ground. The train grew larger and larger in my field of vision. I could see the motorman quite clearly (although not his face), and he made no movement of any kind. The crowd was shouting now, their yells and cries bouncing off the tiled walls of the station, building to a great roar as the train approached the amphibian man. Twenty yards. Ten yards. The train slowed to a crawl, but continued forward. The shouting stopped in an instant. Five yards. The amphibian man leaned forward as he waved. It seemed impossible to me that the motorman had made no sign, no movement. The train reached the man, and very slowly began to fold him over.

Suddenly a dozen people jumped down onto the tracks —businessmen, students, a few young women. They pushed at the front of the train and beat the glass panel with their arms and fists. The train stopped, and now the pale, expressionless moon-faced visage of the motorman could be seen as he leaned forward and pressed against the glass.

The amphibian man was pulled out from under the car, filthy, but unhurt. His overnight bag had been caught under the wheels and destroyed. It hung at his side like an eviscerated animal. The doors to the train sighed open, and there was an instantaneous reversal in the mood of the crowd. People climbed up from the tracks laughing. The amphibian man tried to brush the dirt from his trenchcoat, and gazed ruefully at his overnight bag. Everyone boarded the train as if nothing had happened. I followed.

The local transit authority memorandum mentions a rowdy crowd of inebriates on the tracks for no apparent reason, and sidesteps the issue of the two-and-a-half-hour wait. I have some sympathy for the man who wrote it— after all, when things are inexplicable it is sometimes better to invent—and civic trust in the system is essential. I said nothing in my report to contradict the memorandum, but the facts are as I describe them here. I have been haunted, for months now, by the feeling that the incident at M—— is some kind of message, some kind of coded, whispered message that I should be able to figure out, but can't.

Yours,

E. WOREL

GOSSIP

It was ten P.M. on a Wednesday night in 1966 when George paid the cab driver and stepped out onto the sidewalk in front of McShane's Bar & Grille. A tall, thin young man, slightly stooped, slightly pigeon-toed, with an odd narrow face unmarked by age or worry lines, a face so smooth and youthful it seemed that life must never have touched him. His face may thus have represented, by some hidden chemistry, the power of his will, since the method he had used to deal with pain—of which he had had his full human share—was denial. He did not deny pain's existence, but only its power over him. (In this, he was of course mistaken.) He was twenty-eight, intelligent, and ignorant of the forces that moved him. More than most young men, he was entranced by the surface of life, not because he was shallow, but because he thought the surface might reveal some hitherto unknown (to him) route of access to the interior, to the inside of life, where he might finally become a man instead of a young man. He wanted an older face.

He felt a pleasant anticipation as he entered McShane's, a writers' hangout, where on any given night he could be sure of meeting a few friends, who, like himself, were unknown artists working on faith. The comraderie of the place was satisfying. It assuaged the sense of loneliness he felt in his marriage, a college marriage he refused to examine out of fear of what he might find. His wife refused to come to McShane's, perhaps for the same reason.

"Giorgio!" McShane, a short, blond, two-hundred-and-sixty-pound homosexual and fellow Irish-American, had for some reason decided early on to call George Giorgio. McShane emerged smiling from the crowd at the bar. "Have a drink," he said, raising a finger for the bartender while leading George back to the space he had himself occupied. "The big table will be free in a minute."

Because he was one of the original group of young writers who had helped establish the place, he was accorded certain favors. He could run a tab for months (McShane always knew when he'd sold a piece of magazine journalism, and did not expect to be paid until then), and was always assured a chair at the big table where the other writers tended to congregate. George was flattered, and the drinks were cheap. He came every other night.

Scotch and soda in hand, George rested the small of his back against the bar and surveyed the room. He saw half

a dozen people he knew, but the special friends he was to
meet had not yet arrived. The Group—Ivan, the painter,
Jean-Claude, the journalist for *Paris Match,* Yolande, the
Eurasian model, Ted, the jazz-pianist, and Bobbie, the Bra-
zilian-American hostess. An outrageously glamorous group,
whose friendship he prized deeply. At dinners, parties, and
social events all over the city he'd had fun with them, more
fun than he'd ever had in his life. He valued fun. It was
much more to him than diversion.

"I had a weird dream, the weirdest dream."

He realized with surprise that Mary Stein, a writer of
about his own age whom he knew slightly, was sitting
beside him, facing in the opposite direction. Her remark was
addressed to him.

"What happened?" He half-turned toward her, while
watching the front door for Ivan and the others.

"I was on the bank of a river, or like the intercoastal
waterway or something and . . . "

George listened abstractedly. Mary was a good writer,
a working-class intellectual, not particularly pretty but de-
cidedly sexy. Recently (although not tonight), she had been
going out with Joshua Barnes, and George admired her
courage. Barnes was a poet, blind from birth, brimming
with repressed anger, and generally neurotic and difficult.
She continued, now, to describe her convoluted and surreal
dream, a dream of which, her tone suggested, she was
slightly in awe. George half-listened, and it was perhaps
precisely for that reason—that he was not so much listening
as monitoring the story unconsciously—that its meaning
came to him complete and fully formed.

"Weird," she said, when she'd finished.

The big table was ready now, and George stood up

fully. "Not so weird," he said, flip, showing off. "It means you're pregnant." He started to move away, aware that she was getting up to go with him, when he glanced at her and stopped.

He'd often read descriptions of people in novels "turning white" or "ashen," and as a writer, he would never have allowed himself to use those words. Not, that is, until he saw Mary actually do it. Her knees seemed about to give way, and he quickly grabbed her elbow. Her body leaned in toward his.

"Don't tell anybody," she said quickly. "Please don't tell anybody."

"It's okay," he said, holding her. "Mary, I'm sorry. I'm very sorry."

"You can't tell anybody. I can't explain, but you . . ."

"Stop. Stop. I promise. Mary, I promise I won't breathe a word. You don't have to explain anything. I absolutely promise."

"My God."

"Come on." He led her toward the big table. "We need to sit down. We need a drink."

She followed his lead and they took chairs next to each other at the otherwise empty table.

"What do you want?"

"What?" Still stunned, she looked at him as if she'd never seen him before.

"Scotch?"

"Brandy. A large brandy." She took a deep breath, looked down at the surface of the table, and slowly shook her head. "Jesus."

The brandy seemed to help her. They sat in silence for

some time, watching the crowd, people coming in and out, waiters slipping through like vertical fish. Eventually another regular joined them, and another, and general conversation began. Mary said something about a movie she'd seen and George felt a sense of relief.

When the group came in he caught Ivan's eye and made a movement with his head to indicate the back of the restaurant. Ivan understood and swept the others along.

George stayed with Mary until, finally, she touched his arm. "I'm okay," she said. "I know you want to join them."

"Are you sure?"

On his way to the back table he unconsciously puffed his cheeks and blew out some air. He sat down with his friends.

"What was that all about?" Ivan asked.

"Nothing, nothing."

He kept his promise, and told no one. For a week or so the incident would pop into his mind now and then. The strength of Mary's reaction surprised him. She would have Joshua Barnes' child, and presumably they'd get married before, or after, or perhaps never. It was the sixties, after all, so what was the big deal? Maybe she hadn't told Joshua. Maybe he'd get angry. Maybe his blindness was a factor. George came to see there was no way to know what might be involved. He liked to think Mary was simply old-fashioned. Ivan, a fast-living bachelor, had accused George of being too conservative about sex, a bit square, even, and George knew it was true. It was nice to think other people might be square as well.

After two or three weeks he'd forgotten the whole episode. It was as if it hadn't happened.

A year later George's book came out. Modest sales but a critical success. He was dizzy with happiness. He did not, however, feel any older. Despite years of hard work and hard drinking, he still looked, and to some extent felt, like a kid out of college.

Ivan had a show at an important gallery and sold every piece. Yolande signed a design contract with a big fashion house. Jean-Claude's translation of a new American play was a hit in Paris, and Bobbie's invitations were more sought after than ever. All this worked to bring the group closer together, as if they needed each other to understand what was happening. In truth, they didn't understand much. They were having fun. It was that time of life for them.

When someone offered them a free house in the Caribbean for ten days, they accepted instantly. They invited two other people who got reservations at nearby hotels—Harriet Brement, the famous playwright, a tough old woman who seemed to be amused by them, and Susan Strand, an actress from their own generation. George's wife didn't want to go.

"Listen," Ivan said. "Why do you think she came?"

"For this!" George swept an arm to indicate the great bowl of clear sky, the blue-green Caribbean, the sun. They'd been diving from the rocks, and now sat resting on the volcanic basalt, ocean on one side, swimming pool and chiseled stone steps up to the house on the other.

"Why did you invite her, then?"

"Me? I thought *you* invited her, that night we went down to hear Ted sit in with Zoot Sims."

"It was you."

"It was? Okay. So? She understood it was a whole gang. It wasn't like . . . "

"George," Ivan interrupted, "are you going to leave her all alone in that hotel every night? While you come back here to your little room?"

George laughed. "Hey. I've never touched her. She's a pal."

"Why do you think she went to the Lido? Why isn't she over at the Caravanserie talking theater with Harriet?"

"Anyway, I'm married."

Ivan smiled and turned to look out at the ocean. "Okay, my friend," he said gently.

George turned his back to the sun, lay down on the hot, smooth rock, and looked down at the swimming pool. Yolande and Bobbie were in the water. Jean-Claude sat on the diving board. Near the shallow end, Harriet and Susan sat at a white table under a white umbrella, sipping tall drinks. When people moved, they moved languidly. George watched through half-closed eyes, and drifted into sleep.

By the second day patterns seemed to have emerged spontaneously—at the beach by late morning, back for naps in the late afternoon, communal dinners in the big house, the Casino until closing, and everyone to bed. Jean-Claude prepared the big lunch basket. Ivan—a compulsively neat man—kept the house clean. Yolande and Bobbie made splendid dinners, and George was responsible for transportation in the rented car, picking up Harriet and Susan, dropping them off, getting the groceries. They all took quiet pleasure in this effortless cooperation.

Conversation at dinner was fast, all seven people

drinking wine, laughing, and pushing the badinage. There were no subgroups, but a continuous game of verbal Ping-Pong with a couple of balls constantly in motion, everyone participating.

"To beauty!" Ivan, slightly drunk, raised his glass.

"Yes!"

"Abso-fucking-lument!" George said.

"No, no. It's absolu-fucking-ment," Jean-Claude said.

"Who was it," Harriet rasped through cigarette smoke, "who refused to drink a toast to art? I can't remember."

George watched Ivan pour more wine. Why, he wondered, was Ivan so eager to get him into Susan's bed? The Group had always kept sex more or less out of the picture. Jean-Claude and Yolande lived together, Ivan and Bobbie had been lovers long ago but no longer were, and there was a tacit agreement that the Group itself was more important than sex, that, indeed, it provided a kind of relief from those forces, a kind of comfortable free-zone based on another, calmer kind of love. George decided it was only Ivan's campaign against George's squareness coming up again. Ivan, his round, vaguely eskimolike face glowing from many glasses of Medoc, seemed genuinely only to want everyone to have a good time. George felt a surge of affection for him.

Crammed into the car on the way to the Casino, they sang songs—old songs like "Moon Over Miami," or "Harbor Lights," as well as Beatles tunes. Susan's voice was clear and on pitch and she knew the words to everything. She sat next to George in the front seat, leaving Harriet the window, and he could feel the warmth of her breath as she sang. It was her idea to do a substitution of the word lunch for love, as in "I Can't Give You Anything But Lunch, Baby," "Lunch for Sale," "Once I Had a Secret Lunch," etc., which they all sang in a mood of increasing hilarity.

Under the headlights, a black, liquid movement across the coral road.

"What was that?" Harriet threw out her cigarette and pushed the lighter to start another.

"A mongoose," said George.

"Almost like a snake, that movement."

In the car they never played the radio. They did not, for this time, want to hear about Vietnam, or the various evils loose in the United States. Even Harriet—Communist in the thirties, Marxist-Leninist today—didn't want to hear about it and didn't want to talk about it. A mongoose across the road could stop their singing in an instant, but it was only an interruption, a moment to recognize and then pass over.

The Casino was very small (a roulette table, two craps tables, two card tables, and slot machines lining the walls), and was managed by three middle-aged Americans, all from the South, who had the demeanor of friendly plainclothes cops. They instantly recognized Harriet and Susan, and went out of their way to make sure the entire group knew they were welcome.

"You shouldn't play roulette," George said to Ivan. "The odds are better at dice."

"I don't care about odds. Roulette is more interesting to the eye. I like the gaudiness. I like the way the ball pops around."

Harriet played twenty-one in a haze of cigarette smoke, never moving from her seat, croaking "hit me" or "stay" at the black dealers, her old, creased, pendulous Jewish face showing no expression whether she won or lost. Ivan played roulette impulsively, varying his method of betting on whim, scattering chips here and there. George played craps rather cautiously. Yolande, Bobbie and Jean-Claude roamed about, occasionally placing bets. Susan didn't bet at all. She often stood with George, throwing the dice for him, or suggesting a break at the bar when he was losing. She was full of wit, and seemed to enjoy making him laugh.

Sometimes the American staff would invite them to stay after closing. They'd drink champagne, and if they'd lost, Susan would parody their state of mind by crawling along the floor under the slot machines looking for quarters. She'd find them, too, and bring them back to George, whispering, "Here's our stake for tomorrow. We'll break these bastards yet."

One night, as he drove Susan home, she began horsing around. It was a reënactment, she said, of a scene she'd played in a movie. She mussed his hair, kept a line of monologue running about something from the plot he didn't understand (he'd never seen the movie), blew in his ear, and generally vamped him.

"Hey!" He laughed, pulling the car off the shoulder back onto the road. "We'll crash!" She stopped. She'd been goofing, of course, but he'd felt her power, the perfect control over her voice, her body, the tempo of events. He was simply no match for her, and he knew it.

"Let's stop," she said. "Over there, by the pier. I want to look at the water."

He pulled off the road and they got out of the car. Susan skipped ahead.

"Isn't this gorgeous?" She held her arms aloft.

Indeed it was. A warm, clear night. Stars. The lights of her hotel across the little bay shining steadily, the reflections of each point of light rocking in the black water. He stood with his back against a piling. She walked up the pier a little way, and then came back. She wore a white cotton dress and white shoes. As she joined him, he saw that she was smiling. She raised both arms and clasped her hands behind his neck. Her touch seemed almost supernaturally light.

"I understand," she said, kissing him, "that we must exercise the utmost discretion." Another soft kiss. "I can assure you," she said, pressing him gently against the piling, "that I'm good at discretion."

His hands went automatically to her hips. He was momentarily at a loss for words.

"Don't you want to?" she asked, her hands moving up to cradle the back of his head. The pupils of her brown eyes seemed enormous.

"Yes." He gathered her in. "I want to."

They made love that night in her hotel room. For the rest of their time on the island they made love every day —either in the afternoon, or at night—and managed to hide it from everyone. At the beach, at dinner, at the Casino, their behavior toward each other was, to all outward appearances, the same as before. George was astonished. "Are we really fooling them?" he asked one afternoon as they lay, naked and glistening, on her bed. "Or are they just letting us think that we're fooling them?"

"I think we're fooling them," she said.

He was very careful, and yet he couldn't quite believe it. Aware that he was obsessed with her, and profoundly moved by the fact that she wanted him as much as he wanted her, cleansed, lightened, and glowing as he was, it seemed impossible his friends had noticed nothing.

The morning before the last day, they went to a new beach, on the far end of the island, all save Harriet, who was too hung over, and chose to remain in her hotel. They explored, swam, collected shells in groups of two or three, and eventually drifted back to the picnic basket at midday.

"One more swim before lunch," Yolande said. "Anybody?"

"You're on." Susan got up from her towel.

The others watched as the two women ran into the water. Susan kicked spray on her way to the deep water, dove cleanly, and disappeared.

"Well," Ivan said. "You blew it, George. Life passes, and you let it pass."

"*Tais-toi, imbécile,*" Jean-Claude said.

George lay down on his back and closed his eyes. There was silence.

Bobbie spoke. "Not everybody is like you, Ivan," she said.

George thought he should say something, but he felt too many conflicting emotions. Guilt, that he had fooled his friends, accompanied by satisfaction, a feeling of safety. He didn't like the satisfaction—it seemed tinged with smugness. He knew, he had known all along, that his time with Susan would end when they left the island, so it seemed both easier and better to say nothing.

The end of the sixties marked a period of great change for George—all crammed into a year or two, like the playing out of some cabalistic, mystical prophecy—and the changes frightened him profoundly. His marriage ended and he left the house with a hundred and thirty dollars, no job, and little confidence that he could ever write another book. His depression was intensified by the after-effects of having gone, twice weekly, for six months, to a corrupt doctor who adminstered intravenous vitamin B12, B complex, calcium gluconate, and methamphetamine. The Group had broken up. Jean-Claude left Yolande and returned to Paris. Ted moved to California to do movie scores. When Ivan became Yolande's lover, George knew it was all over. He left the city and moved to a small town on the coast of Maine. After several years he married a local girl, and eked out a living doing magazine journalism by mail, and hard physical labor on the fishing boats.

In the early seventies he went to New York to interview a famous poet for a piece in *Esquire*. At a cocktail party in the poet's loft, he bumped into Mary and Joshua Barnes. Mary left her husband's side as soon as George entered, approaching him with an odd expression, at once dreamy and intense.

"I was told you might be here."

"You were?" he said stupidly. He wondered what was going on. Her eyes seemed locked on his.

"It was a girl, you know," she said.

For a moment he was at a loss, and then he remembered the night at McShane's. "Oh, that's wonderful," he said, and smiled. "Terrific."

Now her expression was slightly quizzical, as if he had some important knowledge and she had to find a way to get it out of him.

"My life is completely different now," he found himself saying. "I haven't been in New York for years."

"I know that." She led him over to Joshua. "Josh. It's George, visiting from the wilderness."

"Hi, Josh."

Josh turned his blind, rigid face toward the source of the sound. "The dream reader. Hello, George."

They made small talk, with Mary hovering silently, watching them. George was uncomfortable—he sensed some subtle animus in Josh, a faint pressure under the surface of the words, and he moved away as soon as he could.

The hard winter of 1978 began early in Maine. Heavy snow in November, dark skies, constant wind. George tried to write in the bedroom of the partially heated house. His wife, Kate, worked as a waitress in a local restaurant. They were three thousand dollars in debt—not that much for George in the old days (which seemed to him truly another life, a previous incarnation), but a great deal now.

One night he sat in the kitchen with a beer, waiting for Kate. The faucet was set to drip so the pipes wouldn't freeze, and he could see his breath in the air. She entered all in a rush, slamming the door behind her against the wind. A small woman with a sharp, mobile face which seemed to him the personification of alertness and intelligence. A lively face, full of optimism. She was fourteen years his junior. She moved quickly, slipping off boots, scarf, and her puffy, down-filled jacket.

"I got an interesting phone call today," George said.

"A book review?" Stowing the boots. Getting slippers.

"No. A university in Kansas. They want me to go out there and teach a semester."

She looked up. "Teach? I thought you said you didn't

want to teach." Her voice was neutral, as if she needed more information before committing herself to a response.

"That was literature. This is writing. It's because of my book. They want me to teach writing."

"Is that possible? I mean, can people be taught?"

"I don't know."

"How much? Did they say?"

"Thirteen thousand."

"What?" She sat down, and then immediately stood up. "Thirteen thousand?" Her surprise gave way to a sudden smile. "My God. The light at the end of the tunnel. When do we go?"

It took them five days in Kate's old Volkswagen, George driving carefully through the wind and snow. All through the northeast, the radio kept talking about the winter of '78 in portentous tones.

"I don't see why they go on like that," Kate said. "It isn't *that* bad."

In the mountains, he began worrying about the car. The engine was worn, and even a modest grade forced him to gear down and crawl along at thirty miles an hour. They stayed in inexpensive motels, and ate roadside food. At a Howard Johnson's an elderly waitress thought Kate was his daughter, and Kate immediately began improvising dialogue for the occasion.

"Daddy, you promised," she said, embracing her role. "I did all my homework in study hall, and you promised." She was good at it. A natural actress.

"Okay," he said for the waitress's benefit. "But back by ten P.M. or you're grounded."

At the cashier's desk, waiting to pay, he glanced at

himself in the marbled mirror wall. "Do I look that old?"

"I was all bundled up," Kate said, laughing. "My head is small."

He was forty, and he suddenly realized he looked it. Graying hair, lines in his face, a bit jowly. Eight years in Maine, and he'd jumped from college kid to middle age, without the intervening stages.

As the Great Plains began, they passed enormous trailer-trucks spun off the interstate into the snow—some of them damaged, their cabs at odd angles, some lying on their sides in a parody of sleep, some simply abandoned. The sky cleared and bright sun snapped the cold air. The Volkswagen rattled away at a steady fifty-five into Kansas. They arrived at the university residences at midnight, too tired even to notice their surroundings, their bodies still humming from the car as they fell into bed.

George had been teaching for two weeks—seventeen graduate students in a seminar workshop. He sat in his office one morning stapling Xeroxed pages of Stendhal into seventeen piles when someone knocked on the door.

"Come in."

Immediately—simply by the way she entered, her carriage, her first few words—he felt he understood something about her. She was aware that she was beautiful—tall, a great fall of coppery hair, large green eyes, straight nose, generous mouth—but her manner suggested that all that was irrelevant. She wore voluminous clothing in a slightly dated peasant style, as if to hide herself. Her small waist, perfect shoulders, and elegant neck could not, however, be hidden. She sat down and spoke directly, without hesitation, an old leather briefcase on her lap.

"I started off doing poetry," she said. "That's how I got in the program. But now I want to do prose. I've heard how you run your workshop—going line by line—and I want to transfer in." She was in her early twenties, and spoke with a very slight Canadian accent.

"Who are you working with now?"

"Joshua Barnes. He's good, but as I say, I want to do prose." (George had been surprised to find Joshua teaching a semester here. Mary had stayed in New York, but Josh was in Kansas with his daughter Amy, who was now ten years old.) "I know you don't have much time," she said, opening the briefcase. (In fact he had a good deal of time.) "Could you read some of my stuff? I'll come by tomorrow if that's okay." She placed a couple of chapbooks and some manuscripts on the desk.

She was all business, this one, and just a bit pushy. Nevertheless, they were paying him to teach—a responsibility he took seriously—and she was a student, eager to work.

"Okay," he said. "Sure."

She thanked him and left, closing the door behind her.

He lighted a cigarette, turned in his swivel chair, and stared out the window. Students moved along crisscross paths in the snow. The glass windows of the library building shone in the sun. A peaceful scene, in which he took pleasure. After a while he turned back to his desk, and reached for her manuscripts.

At the end of the day he dropped in on the director of the program. "Who is this," he looked down at one of the stories to find her name, "Joan Lavin?"

"Ah, yes. Joan."

George held up the papers. "This is incredibly good stuff."

"Yes. I know."

"She wants to transfer into my class."

"Entirely up to you," the director said. "I don't know much about her. She's from Ontario, I think. She's on scholarship. Very serious." He paused for a moment. "She was living with another graduate student last year. He was finished, but she had a year to go. He did everything he could to get her to go with him, but she wanted to stay and work. I admire that."

George waited, but the director would not say more. "Well, then. I'll tell her it's okay," George said.

George felt himself drawn into the work of teaching by forces which seemed as natural and undramatic as gravity. In his more or less spontaneous analyses of stories in class, he was forced to articulate opinions about how language functions on the page, forced to talk about beliefs he had held for twenty years, with regard to writing, and had never shared, or ever dreamed of testing in debate. He discovered the depth of his suspicion of the abstract, and his concomitant reliance on the actual. The students were intelligent and articulate, and the seminars were nicely unpredictable, never seeming to fall into a pattern. Weak stories, of which there were many, did not dishearten him since they often gave rise to the most spirited discussion.

Joan Lavin tended to be rather quiet in class, measuring her remarks on the other students' work with care. She was inevitably direct, and fair-minded, eschewing intellectual games, and although George sensed a suggestion of distance between her and the others (based on what? he wondered. The fact of her being so far ahead as a writer? Her physical beauty?), they obviously respected her. He wondered if she felt isolated, or lonely, and was immediately irritated at himself for the banality of the speculation. It was none of his business, in any case.

She wrote more material than could be covered in class and so they would meet in his office at the end of the week. (A couple of other students did this also, but none with such regularity.) Side by side at his desk, each with a copy of whatever she had written, they would work through the prose, with George doing most of the talking.

"Now this part," he would say. "The beginning is fine, but then you get into trouble. Look how thick it starts getting. All these metaphors. All this gushy romanticism. It seems self-indulgent. It doesn't pull the reader in, it just puts him in the position of watching all this *writing* going on. You see what I mean?"

He was of course aware of her as a woman, most acutely when she would pull her chair up beside his and sit down, her eyes fixing immediately on the page, her long neck bending slightly, the faint, fresh, unscented perfume of her body enveloping him. The first few moments were always a bit discombobulating, but George believed he never showed it. Her concentration was intense, and it quickly formed a sort of shield around her. It was almost as if, once he started talking, he was no longer really there as far as she was concerned. She would stare at the page, correlating his remarks with the written words, utterly attentive and alert, her brain working, and he might as well have been speaking to her over the telephone. If another student knocked, or there was some interruption, it was always a slight shock for them both. She could never entirely conceal her impatience at such moments—making a small sound with her tongue, tapping the surface of the desk with her knuckles, or pushing back her chair.

With Joan, George could work both deeper and faster than with any of the others. He found it completely engrossing. After assuring her of his high opinion of her as a writer, he spent week after week, month after month going after every weakness he could find in her prose, attacking from one direction after another, trying to tear the work apart in front of her eyes. She responded by writing better and better stuff, paradoxically with more and more confidence, until it became difficult for him to find any of the weaknesses she had originally exhibited. The onus shifted, and it became necessary for him to work hard in order to keep up with her, rather than the reverse.

"Why don't you ask her over for dinner?" Kate said one night.

"Here?"

"Joan, and a couple of the other hard workers. The one who did that story you liked about her father."

"Gloria."

"And the boy who does avant-garde stuff."

"Daniel."

George pulled at his chin. "I suppose it's okay. The term is almost over."

"You're so old-fashioned sometimes. Of course it's okay. They'll be flattered, and pleased."

"Well, you know," he said, "teaching. It's probably a good idea to keep the lines drawn. Work is work, and then the personal stuff . . . " He trailed off.

"It's not as if they're kids," she said. "They're my age, almost."

"I suppose so."

Part of his reluctance came from his awareness that

Joan was no longer just a student to him. Despite the fact that in their sessions they had never talked about anything but work, he was undeniably drawn to her. She was important to him, and the degree of importance was a secret which he must keep to himself. Their relationship was based on the tacit understanding that they would remain always in their respective roles of teacher and student, and he needed her enough to want to do nothing to threaten that arrangement. Dinner, small talk, socializing, were full of imponderables, and the prospect made him nervous.

He need not have worried. They came together—four of his students—filling the small apartment with energetic chatter, laughter, and a general sense of fun. As it turned out they were all friends, part of a sort of subgroup of the prose students, comfortable with each other and full of gossip about the program. Kate and Joan began preparations for dinner, instantly easy with each other, allied in a mysterious feminine chemistry. George felt a twinge of jealousy, but also a feeling of relief. Everyone seemed to know how to behave, what to do.

After dinner George was flattered when Gloria and Daniel made mention of his book—they were talking about kids and bicycles, which led them to a scene at a drive-in movie from George's book.

"I loved it that the kids got in free," Daniel said. "Was that from life?"

George nodded. "It was smart of the owners. They never could have kept us out. We were like monkeys." After four glasses of wine, George felt impulsive. "Isn't there a drive-in on the edge of town? I love drive-ins. Why don't we go?" He turned to Kate. "Let's take the wine. What do you say?"

"In one car?"

"Of course!"

"Well, we can't take the Volkswagen."

"I've got a Ford," Joan said. "It's old, but it's big."

Joan drove, with Kate and George in the front seat, Gloria, Daniel and a boy named Tom in back.

"This is great," George said. "It must be fifteen years since I've been to a drive-in."

"Do we know what's playing?" Kate asked.

"Probably Charles Bronson," George said, taking a sip of wine. "Clint Eastwood. It doesn't matter."

In the back seat, another bottle of wine and a complicated discussion of Ingmar Bergman's relationship to his repertory company.

"It wasn't Bibi Andersson," someone said. "It was Liv Ullman. He was crazy about her."

George felt the comfortable pressure of his wife's shoulder against his own. He was aware of Joan's wrists, her slender hands on the wheel, the sharp profile of her face behind Kate's.

"There it is!" Joan said, easing up on the accelerator.

George leaned forward and peered through the windshield. The marquee, on spindly stilts rising out of the darkness, had a couple of holes in it, and a few missing letters. *The House on Elm Street,* " he said. "Never heard of it."

"A chop movie, maybe," Daniel said.

"Chop? What's that?" George lowered the wine bottle between his knees discreetly. "Karate?"

"No. Blood and gore," Daniel said.

"Like *Texas Chain Saw,*" Gloria said.

"I hope not," Kate said.

"What's *Texas Chain Saw*?" George asked.

But they pulled up at the booth and everyone searched for money.

"Ten dollars a car," George said. "I've got it, I've got it." He gave the money to Joan, who gave it to the attendant, and they drove through. Joan switched to parking lights and they glided into a spot. George hung the speaker on his window, they passed the wine, and settled back to watch the movie, which was already in progress.

First, a sense of disappointment. The last movie George had seen at a drive-in had been *The Great Escape,* a thoroughly satisfying, visually gorgeous action picture featuring Steve McQueen dashing through lush countryside on a stolen Wehrmacht motorcycle. George had been anticipating that kind of experience—where he could sit with Kate and Joan and the students, and they could make fun of Hollywood and enjoy the movie. What he saw up on the screen now was a rather dim, obviously low-budget production about some punks taking over a suburban house and terrorizing the all-American-family inhabitants. The color values were all wrong, the dialogue barely audible, and the camera jumped around dizzyingly. In one shot, the shadow of the microphone boom was clearly visible.

"What is this?" George said.

"Well, it isn't Burt Reynolds," Kate said, and the others laughed.

As the level of violence in the film escalated, George began to feel increasingly uncomfortable. The teenaged daughter was raped, and he felt his face flush. They watched one of the punks force the father's head down over the kitchen stove, pressing his cheek onto a hot frying pan.

"Good Lord," George said over the sound track screams.

Joan looked over at him with a trace of a smile. "Things have changed at the old neighborhood drive-in."

The plot became more surreal. George found himself watching a scene in which the mother of the family lures one of the punks into the bathroom to perform fellatio, and then bites his penis off.

"We don't have to stay," he said. "We can go."

"It's naïve Grand Guignol," Daniel said lightly from the back seat. "Primitive. Like Haitian painting or something. Fascinating. Let's see a bit more."

George had often been irritated by Daniel's faintly supercilious air of cleverness in class, but never to the degree he felt now. Nevertheless, he remained silent. In his confusion, he was afraid that if he chickened out, the students would somehow think less of him. He looked away from the screen, at the other cars. The people in the other cars were like the punks in the movie.

They stayed to the end, in which everyone died in slow motion, and then rode out to the highway in silence. After a few blocks, George sighed. "I'm sorry. My apologies."

"It's okay," the girls said, all at once.

"I feel like I've been lying in the bottom of a public urinal," George said.

Daniel laughed. "Yes. Amazing what an effect they have, isn't it?"

"You mean there are more like that?"

"Sure. Hundreds. They're in drive-ins all over the country."

"I didn't know," George said.

Joan somehow sensed how upset he was. "Don't worry about it," she said. "We've seen it before."

When they got home he took a shower and sat in the darkness at the end of the bed. "What a catastrophe." He felt a slight movement in the bed and turned to find Kate laughing under the covers. "Hey! What's so funny?"

She sat up quickly and touched his arm to reassure him. "It's okay, you know," she said, calming down. "You can make a mistake like anybody else."

During the last month of classes and office sessions the pace of work increased, and George was forced to set aside a short story of his own. More stories were submitted in each class, and more students came into the office for the kind of editing he'd been giving Joan. There were increasing demands on his time and attention, and he made a conscious effort to be available, even for the weaker writers, at the same time as he met with Joan every few days.

"How's it going with Lavin?" The director asked him one day. "I hear you're doing a lot of work with her."

"Very well. She's got talent and she must write ten hours a day, the amount of stuff she brings in. She's gotten better and I've learned a lot about teaching."

"Good." The director nodded. "She speaks highly of you. I'm glad it worked out."

"I should've done this years ago," George said. "I like it. I hate to leave, actually."

"Well, maybe we can get you back sometime."

He began to notice a certain tension in Joan, a kind of general guardedness in class, where she spoke much less than before, and a slightly harried quality in the office meetings. She worked as hard as ever, but at odd moments would seem preoccupied, as if listening for some sound just out of earshot.

"Maybe you ought to ease up a bit," he said one day in the hall outside his office. She looked up in surprise. "You've done a great deal of work," he went on. "Maybe too much. You seem tired."

She turned her face away and looked down the corridor. Students and teachers milled around. "It's not the work," she said. "I've just been here too long. I've got to get out of here."

There was an intensity to the last phrase that took him aback. "But why?"

She hesitated for a moment, and then made a small dismissive gesture. "Oh, it's nothing, really." A couple of undergraduates passed. "All of us in the program, everybody knows everybody, people don't know how good they are, who's going to make it, or get published. There's a lot of competition. It gets a little—" she paused again, "claustrophobic. Sometimes."

"Oh," he said. "Yes. Of course."

"I'll have the new story in by Friday." She walked away.

He went back in his office and sat down. He realized that when she'd said "I've got to get out of here" he'd felt a shock, a moment of panic. It worried him that he had reacted thus. It surprised him.

In the vast Student Union building, on his way to the bookstore, George stopped to watch as a crowd of undergraduates gathered around a barber-shop quartet from one of the fraternities. Four boys sang "My Blue Heaven," in straw hats, while two of their frat brothers sold tickets to some upcoming event. The sweet, simple harmonies echoed from the walls and ceiling.

"Incredible, isn't it?" The director said, a bundle of files under his arm, obviously on his way to a committee meeting somewhere. "Everything comes 'round again."

"Yes," George said.

"I have to remind myself. This lovely, quiet college town, all the kids like something out of a Frank Capra movie. Ten years ago, right out there," he pointed through the great doors to the quad, "National Guard, riots, tear gas —the works."

"Of course," George said apologetically. "I'd forgotten. It was bad here, wasn't it?"

"It was awful," the director said, and then smiled as he moved away. "I prefer proms and football rallies. I adore Frank Capra, to tell the truth."

George made his way down the wide main hall, passing the video game arcade (electronic rumbles, explosions of quick white noise, the sound of giants marching, ironic, mocking little melodic phrases, twitters, squeaks, zaps—an electric madhouse), the cafeteria, the TV lounge, the banks of shiny vending machines. He glanced through the glass into the bowling alleys, and stopped. Only one lane was in use. George pushed through the door and stood quite still. Joshua Barnes was bowling, and his daughter, Amy, kept score, hunched over the board like some child-clerk from Dickens.

On the lefthand side of the free area two standing ashtrays had been placed about ten feet apart, one near the left hand gutter, and one back near the scoring table. A taut piece of string ran between them—extending the left hand edge of the alley. Joshua bowled in the traditional manner, except that when his backswing was complete, and his left arm came out for balance, the tips of his fingers made contact with the string. As he moved forward his hand slid along the string with astonishing delicacy, allowing him to orient himself correctly and bowl straight. He threw hard, and remained motionless at the foul line, bent over, his ear cocked for the sound of the ball rolling down the alley. As the pins crashed, he straightened up.

"The four and the seven," Amy called out, naming the pins still standing.

As the ball returned, Joshua moved to the right, picked it up as it emerged from the gate, raised it to the right side of his chin, and walked back to throw again. His movements were crisp, almost military.

He threw again, listened with intense concentration, and made a quick, impatient gesture with his shoulders as the ball thumped into the heavy back curtain.

"To the right?" he asked.

"By two inches," Amy answered, her pencil moving in her fist, her head down.

Joshua went to the gate for the ball. George backed up slowly. He wanted to get out before Amy became aware of him. He did not want Josh to know he had watched. For a moment Josh's head turned, as if he had heard something. George slipped out.

Joan did not come to the last two classes, nor did she come to his office. He found himself reacting with a mixture of anger and sadness, and it was the very complexity of his mood that kept him from picking up the phone to call her and find out what was going on. He had learned how to teach with Joan, he had, rather late in life, become a teacher, discovered a new kind of work which he enjoyed and which gave him strength—and yet it was precisely that role, or his understanding of it, that forced him now to accept her actions without question. If she didn't come, she didn't come. She had done far more work than anyone else, and perhaps (though he didn't like to think it) she had no more to learn from him.

He concentrated on the other students and tried not to think of her. But he found himself hoping he would bump into her in the halls. He didn't.

On the last day he and Kate packed up the Volkswagen (new clutch, overhauled engine, new tires), and stopped off at the English department building on their way out of town.

"I'll only be a second," George said in the parking lot. "I left a couple of books in my office, and I have to turn in the key."

He checked his office, pulling out the drawers a final time, making sure nothing was left on the shelves. When he gave the key to the director's secretary, he asked, "Have you seen Joan Lavin? Is she around?"

"I don't know."

One of the typists looked up from her desk. "She was here right after lunch, picking up those flyers for her reading."

"Flyers?"

"Yes. She had thumb tacks and Scotch tape. I bet she's around the building someplace, putting them up."

He walked quickly through the halls of each floor, and worked his way down to ground level. He was about to give up when he saw her at the inner doors of one of the side entrances, taping up a mimeographed notice.

"Hey," he said. "I was looking for you."

She seemed flustered, glancing at him quickly, then pulling out tape to stick up another notice. "Hi. I guess you're off soon," she said.

"Today. This minute, in fact. The car is outside."

"Oh." She stopped. "Well, you're lucky. Where are you going?"

"Back East. Another teaching job."

She met his eye for a moment. "That's good. You're a good teacher." She turned, and they walked down the hall. At the main doors, she started taping notices, and he felt a surge of irritation. He wanted to say something to her, but he couldn't figure out what it was. He gave a little wave and went through the doors.

"Bye," he heard her call.

In the car, Kate folded up the road map she'd been looking at. "All set?"

"Yup." He started the engine and they drove away.

A year passed. George taught a workshop at Princeton one day a week and worked hard at his writing. Kate had signed up for courses toward accreditation as an X-ray technician. ("I like to see inside," she'd said. "It fascinates me, to be able to interpret the *inside*.") When she found out she was pregnant, she increased her course load. They lived in a small walk-up near the university.

One day the mailman delivered a parcel. It contained a book-length manuscript from Joan, who asked George to read it—almost all of the stories from the workshop in Kansas were included—and tender his advice about the sequence, and any style editing that seemed appropriate. A major publisher had agreed to do the book. George wrote back (to Port Townsend, Washington) with his congratulations, a couple of pages of notes, and the following request:

> *. . . Can you satisfy my curiosity about something? Why were you so eager to leave the Kansas workshop? I heard you turned down a job there. And why did you drop out so abruptly toward the end of the term?*

She answered quickly, thanking him for his notes, and then going on to say:

> *. . . About the other stuff, it seems almost silly now, but it sure didn't at the time. It threw me. I started getting some strange vibrations from the other students, and then some anger from certain quarters, and finally a definite feeling of having been sent to Coventry. I simply couldn't understand what was going on. It was weird. I even went to the university shrink at one point. Finally I wormed it out of Mimi—you remember her? The southern girl who always had so many flowers in her stories? It was gossip. There was gossip going around that you and I were sleeping together. It sounds silly, but it made me so mad I thought I was going to explode.*
>
>   *What I did was find out who Mimi heard it from. Then I went to him, laid out the whole thing, and asked him who he'd heard it from. It took a long time, but I was like a crazy person. Some of them didn't want to tell me, and I had to convince them. I can't remember how many people it was—ten or twelve, anyway—but I finally ran it to ground. It was a girl from the poetry workshop. She cried when she told me. Joshua Barnes had been putting the*

make on her, and she'd said it wasn't right, they were
student and teacher, etc. He said, "Well, look at George
and Joan." And that was where it started. I don't know why
he would say a thing like that . . .

George wrote back:

. . . I'm sorry you had to go through that mess. It doesn't
sound silly to me, it sounds like a nightmare. I believe I
understand most of Barnes' motivation. It had nothing to
do with you, but goes back to an incident many years ago,
when I interpreted a dream of his wife's. It's complicated,
but I'm sure that's where the whole thing started.

Kate was angry when he told her.

"That sleazy son-of-a-bitch! I'd like to punch him in
the mouth!"

"I was angry, too," George said, adding gravy to his
meat loaf. "But then I understood. The dream, the way he
must have . . . "

"Fuck the dream! Fuck his motivation!" She slammed
her flat palms on the table, making everything bounce. "It's
women that take the shit! Look at how she had to go around,
getting it out of them, God damn it!"

"Kate, I know you must . . . "

"Oh, shut up," she cried and there were sudden tears
in her eyes. "What do you care? You're probably *flattered,*
you probably think it's *great* all those people thought you
were sleeping with her. Right? Am I right?"

Later, lying in bed, their bodies not touching, he told
her about his affair in the Caribbean, and the gossip that he
had *not* been sleeping with Susan, that, also, he had been

faithful to *her* throughout their marriage, and that even if he were a tiny bit flattered, somewhere deep, the thoughtless reaction of some smooth-faced boy-self he would never be entirely rid of, given all that, when you looked at it, it didn't matter. What mattered was that everyone was connected in a web, that pain was part of the web, and yet despite it, people loved one another. That's what you found out when you got older, he said.

THE SENSE
OF THE
MEETING

Kirby took the train from Washington. He'd bought a book for the short trip to Philadelphia, but it lay unread on the seat beside him as he watched the frozen Chesapeake slipping past. Long vistas of flat ice and distant, wooded peninsulas gave way to quick close-ups of trailer camps, back yards, abandoned factories, junkyards, lumberyards—everything dim under the gray sky, everything mildly ominous and interesting. Kirby was alert, and dispassionate, a middle-aged man thrust, temporarily, out of his routine. It was Friday, and he was not flying home to Boston as usual, to the splendid fuss his young wife made over his return each week, spoiling him;

no, he was on his own, on a train rushing through the world. He was going back to his old Quaker college to see his old roommates, and to watch his son Alan, a senior, play basketball in the Division III league.

The boy had been six or seven when he'd first asked about the game. Kirby brought home a hoop and nailed it to the back wall of the house. He gave the boy a ball and forgot about it. (Another life! Another wife! Another house, another time, so long ago.) It was a year before Alan got his father to play Horse one evening. Kirby had loved basketball in grade school, but he'd been too thin and weak to play well. By high school he'd given up all sports and spent his time reading. In college, still grotesquely thin, he'd gotten a medical release from athletics. It had been, he later realized, a bad mistake. He'd missed out.

"Okay," he said, bouncing the ball slowly, standing six feet from the basket, "one shot you should learn is the hook. You'll be tall, but probably pretty light, and with a good hook you won't have to tangle with the big heavy guys guarding you. You won't have to go through them, you can go over them." Kirby put his back to the basket. "It works like this." He moved with exaggerated slowness. "You turn, thusly. See, I'm not facing the basket, so the guy can't do much." Alan was all attention, rapt, even, with the special solemnity of extreme youth. "See, I'm exactly side-ways, protecting the ball, and an imaginary line across my shoulders points directly at the basket. Got it?" Alan nod-ded, glancing quickly at the hoop, and then back again. "You hold the ball out here, all the way out your right side, see, even farther away from him, and then, using that imagi-nary line to guide you, you hook it up over your own head, over the other guy, to the goal." Kirby swung his arm up slowly, gave a flick of his wrist, and heard a swoosh. He tried to show no surprise at the ball having gone in. He looked at Alan and saw a complex expression of pleasure, pride, and eagerness on the boy's face. For some reason it was at that precise moment that Kirby understood the force of his son's love. He also felt, for the first time, a flicker of fear that he might somehow, without meaning to, hurt the boy by failing him. It had been, after all, an extremely lucky shot.

Approaching Philadelphia, the train slowed. Kirby stood up in the aisle and got his coat, scarf, and gloves from the overhead rack. Swaying, he put them on and moved to the end of the car. Then he remembered he'd forgotten his book. It was a paperback thriller, and he decided to leave it for someone else. There would not be much time for reading until he got home, in any case. The train stopped in Thirtieth Street Station and Kirby stepped off and moved to the escalator. It was chilly as he glided upwards. At the top he caught sight of Gus moving forward to meet him, his six-foot, six-inch frame easy to spot. Kirby had not seen Gus for ten years—the tall man was a bit heavier, his face a bit rounder, and there were bags under his eyes, but for all that he looked younger than Kirby—a reversal of the old days.

"You made it," Gus said.

Kirby gave him a one-armed hug as they moved towards the exit. He had to reach up to do this, which was unusual, since he was himself tall. He had to reach up to Alan, also. "It's been too long."

"Yes." Gus gave a little laugh and mumbled something. He was a scientist, from a rather strict German-American upbringing in the Midwest, and often mumbled, or made elliptical remarks half to himself, and did not show emotion easily. He seemed always to have some private agenda, some interior activity going on in his head apparently unrelated to the situation in which he found himself, which gave him a slightly distant air. Kirby understood this, and was not put off by it.

They left the station and walked across the parking lot to Gus's Saab. Kirby checked his wristwatch.

"How're we going to do this? I told Alan to be in his room at seven. I promised him a steak dinner."

"Charley is waiting for us." Gus got in.

Kirby got in. "Where?" The car was comfortable, almost luxurious.

"The Hunt Club. Where the lawyers go." Gus pulled out of the lot onto the street. "It's not far, except I don't know how to get there with these God damn one-way streets." He craned his long neck and peered this way and that through the windshield, driving slowly.

"Good. But I'll have to get out to the college somehow."

"Relax," Gus said. A truck pulled in front of them.

"How is Charley?" Charley was their ex-roommate. "Is he doing all right?"

"Very much so. Big top-floor office. The Philadelphia lawyer. Big bucks."

"Good," Kirby said.

"He may talk about his mid-life crisis, however."

"Why? What's wrong?"

Gus gave a small sigh. "Let him tell you." He slowed down. "A left here? Or should I go around?" he mumbled to himself, showing his irritation.

The Hunt Club was small, masculine, and posh. Charley wasn't there yet and they stood at the bar in their coats. They ordered shots and beers, as they had invariably done thirty years ago at O'Rourke's, the college hangout. Gus had been captain of the basketball team and Kirby the editor of the literary magazine, and yet, as if in defiance of the prevailing customs, they had been roommates and friends for three of their four college years.

"So," Kirby said, clinking glasses, "what about you?"

Gus made a dismissive gesture with his free hand. He ignored the question, and shifted the subject back to Kirby. "I read your book when it came out, and I thought, okay, he's used everything up. How's he going to write anything again? I was worried about you."

Kirby drank some beer, looked at Gus and smiled. "I know a wise old poet who lives in New Hampshire. He says try to use everything up every time. Then you regenerate, he says." Kirby leaned forward for emphasis. "How about you? What's happened?"

"Here comes Charley," Gus said.

At college, Charley had been thin and nervous, affected with almost constantly trembling hands. His speech had been unnaturally fast and clipped. Now, as they shook hands, pounded shoulders, and talked, Charley was self-possessed, steady, and well-spoken. He had become quite handsome. His intelligent eyes revealed amusement as he watched Gus stage-manage the move to the table. Unfolding his great crane-like body, Gus mumbled and sighed, elbows stabbing the air, grimacing, gesturing—always managing to keep himself the center of attention. Kirby's and Charley's eyes met in tacit recognition. That's how he is, was the message, and we put up with it. We even encourage it.

"We've missed you," Charley said. "You ought to move down here to Philadelphia and we can do this all the time."

They raised their beers.

Sometime later, Kirby glanced at his watch. It was twenty of seven. "Jesus, I've got to get out there. The boy's waiting in his room."

"Call him," Gus said. "Charley made reservations here. He can come in."

"His car isn't working," Kirby said. "Charley, I'm sorry. I haven't seen him since August."

"Call him," Gus said.

"Let's drive out there and find someplace to eat," Kirby said. "Or I'll get a cab if you guys can't come, but you have to come. He's heard all about you."

"I'll call," Gus said. "Give me his number and . . . "

"Gus," Charley interrupted. "Listen to yourself." He touched Gus's arm. "He's talking about his son. We do not have a problem here. I'll cancel the reservations. I've got my car, you take Kirby in yours, pick up the boy, and we'll meet at a restaurant."

"You're a prince," Kirby said with relief.

"There aren't any restaurants out there. You can't get a decent meal." Gus waved for another round.

"There's got to be a steakhouse," Kirby said.

"Tell you what," Gus said to Charley. "We'll meet at O'Rourke's and figure it out from there."

Charley smiled. "Fine."

"Great," Kirby said. "We've got to chug these drinks, though."

Kirby found Alan's room with a minimum of trouble. The dorm had the same exterior as when Kirby lived there, but with a different layout inside. He knocked at number eleven, and heard Alan's voice. He pushed the door open and there was his son, a tall, slender young man sitting, knees high, on a low couch, reading a magazine on a coffee table. Alan looked up, with a slow, familiar smile. "You made it."

"I'm sorry I'm late," Kirby said. "You must be starving."

Alan got up, moving with characteristic languidness.

"Gus is waiting in the car outside," Kirby said.

Alan seemed abstracted for a moment.

"What's wrong?"

Alan picked up his jacket from the arm of the couch. "Nothing. It's okay." He gave a little fatalistic laugh. "It took me two hours to clean the place up." He looked around. "I can hardly recognize it myself."

Kirby felt guilty, and walked across the small, sparsely furnished room. "Hey. It looks great. Fireplace. This is great." There were two doors to the side. Kirby pointed at one. "Your bedroom?"

"That's Steve. My roommate. He's not here now. The other one is mine." Alan put on his jacket. "Okay. Let's go."

"You look like you put on a few pounds," Kirby said. "You look terrific."

He was relieved to get out of the room. He didn't understand what came over him sometimes when he saw Alan on Alan's own turf, a great rush of bittersweet, protective love, a desire to shelter the boy against some vague, unnamed threat. Kirby knew his reaction was inappropriate, perhaps even dangerous, and yet, often, he couldn't control it. His young wife had pointed out that Alan was strong and smart, and did not need any protection, and Kirby knew this was true. Yet why, when he saw his son sitting in a dorm, reading a magazine, or standing in the sun in his carpenter's garb on the roof of a half-finished house with a hammer in his hand, or playing solitaire in a train station waiting room, or talking to a girl on the sidewalk of the town they went to every summer—why, when he saw these images from a slight distance, so that he, Kirby, was apart from what he saw, did he feel as if his heart would break? His wife, exactly halfway between them in age, said it was because Alan was growing up, becoming a man. Kirby could not quite believe it, and yet had no explanation himself. It remained a mystery.

O'Rourke's was a small, dark, working-class roadside bar a half-mile from the college. It looked very much the same as when Gus, Kirby, and sometimes Charley had shot darts there years ago.

"Not so many college kids come," Alan said.

"Why not?" Kirby asked. The place had symbolic value to him—it was imbued with memories of youth.

"Because they hate us," Alan said without rancor. "Carding people all the time. Bitching when we order food. Putting us way in the back."

"Interesting." Kirby leaned toward the passing bartender. "Four shots of bourbon and four beers."

A brief struggle between Kirby, Gus, and Charley about paying. Kirby prevailed and raised his shot. "Here's to tomorrow's game," he said to Alan. "Hope it's a good one."

"Smash the red-bellies," said Gus.

"Good luck," said Charley.

They drank.

Alan looked at Gus. "Dad said you had the rebound record. I looked it up today."

"Somebody broke it," Gus said.

"But it held for fourteen years," Alan said.

Gus ordered another round. Alan refused the bourbon but accepted the beer. "I'm not all that good a player," Alan said, "but I love the game."

"Well, that's what matters," Charley said. "Doing what you love." He sipped his beer. "What are your plans for next year, after graduation?"

"A job, I guess. If I can get one." He gave a short sigh. "People in my class are incredible. They seem to have their whole lives planned out. Investment banking. Corporate programs. Medical school. They talk about money all the time. Life strategies. I just can't get into it. I don't know what I want to do, except I've had enough of school."

Kirby nodded. "Except you said you might try law school in a year or two."

"Maybe," Alan said. "Yes."

"Good for you," said Charley. "I'm here to tell you that planning it all out doesn't necessarily work."

"Here we go," said Gus, putting down his beer and turning to Kirby. "Darts?"

"In a second. What do you mean? I'm scared to death he'll follow my example. I floated around for years, broke, sorry for myself, producing nothing. When I finally found teaching I was forty years old, for God's sake. The nick of time! I could have saved myself a lot of trouble. I don't want him to go through that." Kirby realized he was feeling the front edge of the bourbon. Gus moved away to the dart board.

Charley acknowledged Kirby's speech. "But there are other risks," he said, looking directly at Alan, who remained attentive. "I did everything I was supposed to. My father said, look, this is the system, and he laid it all out for me and it made perfect sense. Other wise men agreed. Go to law school, then enter here at a certain salary, after so many years you'll be making such and such, and then, if you're good, you'll move up to this level, and then here." Charley was motionless, his voice even. "I've been very successful. I've made a lot of money. But I've worked for other people all my life, meeting other people's needs. I have reacted. I've never done what I wanted to do. I'm terrified because I don't even know if there is anything I want to do. It may be too late. I feel a sense of loss, and I don't even know what I've lost."

Both Kirby and Alan remained silent for a time. Kirby heard Gus behind them, putting in a challenge to get the dart board.

"Yes," Kirby said finally. "You're right. There are risks on both sides. I guess it's because I was flat-out poor, once as a child, and then again in my thirties. It's very hard to climb out of that. Particularly the second time."

"I know," Charley said. "I've been safe all the way through, but I know what you're talking about."

"Christ!" Kirby gave his son a quick squeeze of the hand. "I must sound like some father out of a thirties novel." But Alan seemed to be thinking over what Charley had said.

"I guess it's a question of balance," Alan said to Charley. "One good thing is I'm not worried about my ability to make a decent living. I'm fairly sure I can do that."

"Hey, you guys." Gus broke in, his long arms enveloping Charley and Kirby's shoulders. "Let's go! I got the board. Two teams. Cork before the inning! What do you say, Alan? You up for it?"

"Sure. I'll play with my dad."

They got fairly drunk—except for Alan—and didn't eat dinner until nearly midnight.

The next day, the day of the basketball game, it snowed. Kirby and Gus played a game of chess in the living room of Gus's large, quiet house. Gus's children were away at college, and his wife in bed with the flu. Kirby moved his queen's bishop and looked out the window at the steady fall of snow over the suburban hills.

"I suppose the roads will be all right," he said.

"I've got snow tires." Gus hunched over the board like an enormous mantis. His long hand descended slowly, his fingers touched a pawn and edged it forward, and he mumbled something.

"What?"

"This is a cockamamie opening," Gus said. "Why did I do this?"

"To get my pawn. That's why. You're a pawn up."

"I don't like the position."

Kirby studied the board, and castled. Solid, conservative play. Gus raised his eyebrows theatrically, rubbed his face, moved a little closer, stared down at the pieces for what seemed to Kirby to be an endless amount of time, and then looked up—his startlingly blue eyes pinning Kirby with their intensity. "Too soon, too soon," he whispered, his elbows like wings.

"What?" Kirby re-examined the board, saw nothing.

"Mate in four," Gus whispered.

"What? What?"

Gus demonstrated. A bishop sacrifice. A check with his knight. Queen comes out to check, forcing the black king to bishop one. Knight mates. He collected the pieces in one hand as it roamed over the board, tucking them into his palm like toothpicks.

Kirby laughed, and sat back. "Just like the old days. I suppose we could live to ninety and it wouldn't change."

"I'll settle for eighty-five," Gus said.

"Why don't we go now?" Kirby said. "We can stop for lunch—time things so we're not late."

"Okay. I'll get the keys."

The Saab was a good car in the snow, the front-wheel drive pulling them out of the small drift in the driveway. Their breath fogged the windshield immediately, and Gus slowed to a crawl on the winding street, reaching down to adjust the wipers and the defroster.

"It'll be better in a minute."

"I can't see a thing," Kirby said, rubbing his windows.

"Neither can I." Gus said. "Good thing I know the roads around here."

"Ha! I think I'll buckle up." Kirby strapped himself in and lighted a cigarette.

"I'll take one of those," Gus said.

"I thought you didn't smoke," Kirby said, surprised.

"In the house I don't. Outside, sometimes I do."

They rode in comfortable silence through the suburban maze and out onto a state highway. Kirby felt slightly dreamy, slightly outside of himself—perhaps because he knew that with Gus he could speak freely, an old friend whose life no longer connected with his own. He began to feel that he could do no less than speak freely, since the special circumstances—their having started off together, each going his own way—suggested a special value to whatever they might say to each other. Neither had an ax to grind, both were presumably curious as to what the other had learned, or thought he'd learned. It was a sort of triangulation process, Kirby thought, a navigational urge. He wondered if Gus felt it as strongly as he did himself.

"So what's this with Charley?" Kirby asked.

Gus screwed up his face as if in pain and shook his head slowly. "He says he doesn't know the point of it all."

Kirby waited. He lighted two cigarettes and gave one to Gus.

"I tell him the children are the point," Gus said. "He's crazy about his kids. His son plays the guitar and writes rock tunes, and Charley loves it. He wants his kids to be creative." He put a little spin on the word. "He thinks you and I are creative, that we've done what we want."

"You think children are the point?"

"I don't know. Maybe."

"I can't believe they are. Not the whole point."

They rode in silence for several miles.

"The trouble with Charley," Gus said, "is that he looks for solutions. He wants solutions."

The snow was falling more heavily, and there was a wind now, occasionally buffeting the Saab. They couldn't see very far into the whiteness.

"I had a nice little restaurant in mind," Gus said. "But I'm not sure I can find it in all this."

"Stop anywhere. We'll get a hamburger."

After several more miles a fast-food franchise emerged, coming up quickly like a photograph in a developing tray. Gus pulled in and they ordered from the car.

"I've been working on more or less the same problem for about ten years," Gus said, as they unwrapped the food. "I do the ideas. I come up with ideas, ideas that cut corners with what I hope is a certain amount of elegance. Other people do the actual work. I'm not that good at doing science, the hands-on stuff. I don't have the right personality." He paused to open a little plastic pouch of ketchup with his teeth. "If I run out of ideas, I'll have to do science, and I won't be very good at it."

"That hasn't happened yet, though," Kirby said.

"Not yet."

"What's the nature of the work?"

"It has to do with antibodies. Their genetic structure. We're trying to find out how they recognize self from non-self. Nobody knows at the moment."

"Yes, yes," Kirby said. "I was reading about it, somewhere. You know, for the layman. What was it the guy said? That maybe they don't sense molecules as actual things, but as a sort of humming. A vibration. Self and non-self. It seems as much philosophical as scientific."

Kirby collected all the trash and jammed it into the little white bags. He got out of the car, and, leaning into the wind, made his way over to the plastic garbage can. As he stuffed the bags through the swinging door, his eyes half-closed against the snow, an image came to him. A scene from a golf game the previous summer.

He'd been walking down the fairway with his friend Tom.

"Look at that," Tom had said, pointing at Alan moving along the edge of the fairway. He'd known Alan from the time Alan was nine years old.

Kirby had looked. Alan was gliding along, swinging his club easily. He wore blue jeans cut off just above the knee, and a white short-sleeved shirt.

"Beautiful," Tom said. "Like something from ancient Egypt."

And Kirby had seen it instantly. A tall, slender young man gliding, floating almost, down the grassy incline—his long legs taking effortless strides with that slow African grace we see in the antelope, or the giraffe, his back straight, his broad shoulders high and even, the slender neck, the perfectly shaped head with its mysterious stillness. Kirby saw the demeanor of a pagan prince—he saw his son through Tom's eyes for a moment, as he had never seen him before, and then Alan had ducked, and disappeared into the brush to find his ball.

"Hey!" Gus called through the open door of the car. "It's getting cold in here!"

Kirby turned away from the garbage can and returned to the car. Gus pulled out of the driveway, and the rear wheels broke loose for a fraction of a second as they turned onto the road.

"This can't be Pennsylvania," Gus said, straining to see. "This is Lake Woebegone, Minnesota."

"Can we make it on time?" Kirby asked.

"Relax."

"This basketball thing may have gone too far," Kirby said. "You know how things can creep up? He's only with me summers, and for years, God, even before high school, when we talk on the phone I always say how's the B-ball going until it's just completely ritualized. I mean he may think I think basketball is really important, when all I've been doing is showing an interest in case he thinks basketball is really important."

"Give me a cigarette." Gus held out his hand.

Kirby lighted two. "Love is complicated. It can get in the way, keep you from talking straight. It's weird."

"Don't worry so much." Gus said. "Remember, I was there, where he is. When he's playing he's going to be thinking about a lot more than his old man, believe me."

"I know. I know. It just seems like it's gotten loaded."

They drove slowly. The wind-whipped snow was like smoke over the road. Headlights would appear in the opposite lane, as dim as kerosene lamps, and then the dark shapes of the cars would pass. They had no real sense of movement.

"I feel a sense of regret sometimes," Gus said. "Now they're growing up. My kids are leaving, and I regret the things I should have done with them and didn't."

"Yes. It hurts. All very banal, but it hurts."

In the warm cocoon of the car, they gazed out at the whiteness around them.

The gym was hot, bright, noisy, and swirling with color. The stands, on either side of the gleaming court, were packed with students from both colleges. Banners, signs, flags, and pennants danced in the crowd. A small, informal brass band playing on the home side was drowned out by a great roar as the teams ran onto the court.

"Just made it," Kirby said as they squeezed into place on a high tier. He saw Alan in the center of the court, shaking hands with the officials. Everything seemed to be happening too fast—the tip-off, the players running to one end of the court, back to the home basket, down again, back again. A quick whistle and a turnover. No score yet, no baskets attempted. "What's going on?" Kirby asked, deferring to Gus's greater knowledge of the game.

"Nothing. They're all so pumped up they can't even play. They'll settle down."

Play continued in a scattered fashion. Kirby watched Alan trying to box out a much heavier red-belly under the basket—hips bumping, arms flying, legs tangling—until they suddenly disengaged and Alan moved to the corner.

"He's open," Gus said calmly.

But the pass was to another player at the top of the key, who shot over double coverage, and missed. Rebound to the red-bellies and everyone ran. A quick pick and roll at the far end for two points. A roar from the visitor's side. The movement on the court was so quick that Kirby saw Alan as if in a series of still photographs—crouched before his man, or holding the ball high over his head before passing, or hanging in the air under the basket, or straining into a run on a fast break. The red-bellies scored twice more before the home team sank a set shot. Instant pandemonium. Dozens of toilet-paper rolls flew through the air, streaming white arcs of tissue above the court to drift down over the players. The brass band pumped out the school song as a dozen students rushed to clear the area.

"It's a thing they've been doing for years, now," Gus shouted. "First home basket, out comes the toilet paper."

The game resumed. Alan ran down the sidelines, stopped in the corner, turned, and saw the ball coming toward him. He reached out, the ball came into his hands, and then left them, as if he'd tried to catch it with his fists. Alan's face seemed blank with shock as he watched the ball go out of bounds. A whistle. Movement on the sidelines as the coach, a small, neat black man in a perfectly pressed tan suit, burgundy tie, and gold tie-pin, sent in another player. Alan went to the bench and sat down.

Kirby glanced up at the scoreboard. Visitors 8, Home 2. Time elapsed, four minutes. "He just started! Why'd they take him out?" He blew up his cheeks and puffed out some air in frustration.

The game began to slow down. When one of the visiting players committed a foul—successfully stopping a layup—the crowd started grunting *You, You, You, You,* jabbing their fingers to indicate the player, their combined hooting building in intensity. *You, You, You.* A frightening atavistic chant which seemed to shake the building. It stopped abruptly for the foul shot.

The home team could not seem to get started. The individual players were working hard, but no team rhythm was emerging.

"Scattered," Gus said. "Scattered play."

Each home basket seemed a great victory over difficult odds. The visitors, on the other hand, made points smoothly, working their picks, screens, and give-and-go's without hesitation, all the while controlling the pace of the game. Alan remained on the bench. At the half, the home team was down fourteen points.

"He didn't call any time-outs," Gus said of the coach. "He should have. He should have been talking to them."

Kirby maneuvered himself down through the crowd and caught Alan on his way to the locker room.

"Hey," Kirby said.

"The worst four minutes of basketball I ever played in my life."

"You'll get 'em next half."

Alan gave a little snort. "If he lets me play. I have to go, Dad. Coach will want to talk to us." He walked away toward the doorway where the other players were moving through, heads down.

Gus and Kirby stepped outside the building for a smoke. The snow was tapering off and the wind had dropped. The campus seemed unfamiliar from where they stood. So many new buildings had gone up, Kirby, had he been led blindfolded to the spot, would not have known where he was.

"He's never gotten much playing time," Kirby said. "And of course I always blamed the coaches. That's the way your mind works when you're at a distance. It's easy to do that. But now we're on, what, the third coach in four years, and none of them have played him much. It must be, it probably is—" he hesitated, not wanting to say it, "he isn't a particularly strong player."

"They've had too many coaches," Gus said. "It's bad for team morale."

"Last year he said morale was very low."

"It's important in basketball. That team feeling. It really is."

They re-entered the gym and found their seats. The second half commenced with Alan on the bench, shouting encouragement to his teammates. It remained a lopsided game, and by the fourth quarter the visitor's lead had opened up to sixteen points. Suddenly a home player was on the floor. Kirby had seen no contact.

"What was that? You see anything?"

"No," Gus said.

The player was kneeling now, clearly woozy, the ref

and the trainer leaning over him, each with a hand on his back. After another minute, they led him off the court. Alan was still on the bench as play resumed.

He did not come in until the last five minutes, when the home team was down twenty points. The coach had sent in a play, in which the home team formed two lines on either side of the key, passed the ball back and forth toward midcourt, and ran patterns. Since they were nowhere near the basket, it looked pointless. The crowd took up another powerful chant. Boring, Boring, Boring, Boring, until the ball was stolen. Kirby covered his eyes.

For the remaining time Alan worked at defense, pulled down a couple of rebounds, and scored two baskets—a shaky jump shot from about fifteen feet, and a tip-in under the boards. Most of the time he was simply running, while others handled the ball. When the final buzzer sounded, the game lost, he went to the bench and buried his face in a towel. He sat motionless for several moments. Then he threw the towel to his feet, got up, and went out to shake hands with the winners.

"You know my father died last year," Gus said.

"I didn't know," Kirby said. "I'm sorry." They were sitting in the empty stands, in the nearly deserted gym, waiting for Alan. Kirby remembered Gus's father, from twenty-five years ago, as a difficult man subject to unpredictable mood swings.

"He spoke German in the house, and he had that heavy accent when he spoke English. When I was a kid, after the war, it was very bad to have a German accent. People treated him . . . " Gus's voice trailed off, and after a moment he waved his hand. "At any rate, I was protective of him all through my childhood. Protective. And then later it was important what he thought of me, of my work—the way he'd nod his head when I explained, even if he didn't understand it all." He paused. "When he died I thought, okay, who's going to care what I do now, one way or the other?"

They sat in silence, watching two students collecting papers from the official's table. Someone from the Athletic Department took away the game clock. A black janitor swept up toilet paper ribbons with a wide broom. The bright lights were turned off.

Alan emerged from the side door, saw them, and walked over. He wore blue jeans, a sweater and parka, and he carried a white box in his hand.

"Tough game," Gus said.

"A catastrophe." Alan shook his head slowly.

"The coach kept you quite awhile," Kirby said.

"He chewed us out. He really chewed us out." Alan sat down a tier below them.

"Well," Gus said, "there's the rematch next week. Last game of the season."

"You play them again?" Kirby asked.

Alan nodded. "I don't think anybody's looking forward to it, to tell you the truth."

"Your hands were wood in the first half," Gus said. "But a good job at the end. Good rebounding, good hustle."

"Thanks."

Kirby said, "You were over-revved at the start. You didn't have time to come down."

"I'm glad you guys came, anyway," Alan said. He

gave the white box to Kirby. "I know you have to catch your plane. Here. I got this for you."

Kirby opened the box. It was a letter sweater.

In Boston, at the university co-op pharmacy, Kirby looked down at the counter and the fresh round of drugs his doctor had prescribed as a result of his appointment that morning. A cluster of brown plastic containers of various heights and widths, each filled with pills. Kirby had high blood pressure, an arthritic right hip, a bad knee, and, as he had just learned, mild diabetes.

"God," he whispered.

"Anything wrong, sir?"

"No. Just put them in a bag, please."

At home he felt listless, and found it hard to concentrate on his students' papers. He wore his letter sweater and complained to his wife about the doctor's instructions.

"Two beers a day. No bourbon at all."

"It's not the end of the world," she said. "Suppose he'd cut you off entirely?"

Alan telephoned one evening. "It's gotten down to survival," he said with a rueful laugh. "You remember the kid who fell? Towards the end of the game?"

"Yes. Was he hit? I didn't see it. I meant to ask you."

"No. He fainted. So they've pulled him out. He isn't going to play."

"Fainted?"

"They don't know why. Then yesterday at practice Brian got his jaw broken. An elbow under the boards. You could hear it. The way people are playing in practice, I mean it's crazy. No plays, no teamwork, just a lot of anger. Mitch—the power forward, our best guy—ran into the stands and sprained his ankle pretty bad, so he's out. We're down to six players."

"Jesus."

"He's going to have to bring up some junior varsity for the bench."

"Well, listen, for God's sake be careful. Don't *you* get hurt."

"It's okay."

"I'm coming down for the game."

A brief pause. "Dad, you don't have to do that."

"I want to."

"Chances are, if anything, it'll be worse than last time."

"I'll call Gus," Kirby said. "I'm coming."

It was a different gym—the red-bellies' gym—and a different game. Kirby and Gus sat in the stands, rapt, hardly daring to speak lest they somehow break the spell. Alan was all over the court—setting picks, pulling out the defense for his teammates, threading bounce passes through the middle, occasionally hitting baskets from seventeen or eighteen feet out, jumping in for offensive rebounds. He played his own game—avoiding body contact whenever possible, relying on movement, anticipation and concentration rather than weight and strength—but this time his own game worked. He played smoothly, and never seemed to get rattled when things went wrong. At the half the score was tied, thirty-eight all.

"This," said Gus, "is a hell of a game."

Kirby was tense, his muscles wound tight, his hearing abnormally acute so that he would flinch at each roar, each buzzer. Alan concentrated on team play, searching out opportunities, quietly finding patterns that reinforced the rhythms of the team working as a unit. Kirby knew Alan was hot, and yet the delicacy of it all made him chew his lip.

In the second half Alan, on defense, was switched to cover the other team's high scorer. Kirby and Gus watched him close the man down, holding him to four points in the third quarter. But the man Alan had covered in the first half picked up the slack. Both teams seemed to have entered some special zone of basketball, where the flow of the game was so firm and strong it endowed the players with extraordinary grace, as if they were playing to music only they could hear.

With four minutes to go, down three points after a red-belly foul shot, Alan stood in the key. The ball was about to be put in play. By fluke, all four of his teammates were near him. "Hey!" Kirby heard him call out. "Here! Here!" He held out his hand, palm up, and the others converged, and put their hands on his. "Let's *do* it!" Alan cried, as they broke away.

Kirby thought he had never seen his son so alive, so utterly immersed in life, and the powers of life, as when he shouted those words. And because of what Kirby saw, he felt himself change. He felt a deep shift within himself, and then a release—as all the old love he had felt for Alan flowed away, all the bittersweet love, all the fearfulness of the long-ago hook shot, all the worried love flowed away and evaporated in the heat of Alan's cry. In an instant, a darker, stronger love took its place. This would be the love, Kirby realized, with which they would live henceforth.

Alan's team closed to within one point, with possession of the ball and four seconds to play. The red-bellies put all five men down court, and allowed Alan to make the inbounds pass uncovered. A teammate broke to midcourt, Alan passed to him, the teammate turned, took two steps, and threw a forty-foot, high-arc, jump shot. It hung in the air, descended, and passed through the hoop without a sound. The buzzer went off as it fell from the net.

Alan had a victory party to go to, but he came to O'-Rourke's for a quick one.

"M.V.P.," Gus said, handing him a shot.

Kirby could not have a shot, but he raised his beer. "It was beautiful."

Alan smiled his slow smile. "It sure felt good."

Kirby listened as Gus and Alan discussed the game, reliving various moments, Gus asking technical questions, Alan drawing diagrams in beer on the surface of the bar, turning every now and then to acknowledge a slap on the back from someone in the crowd. The place was noisy, jammed with working-class patrons and celebrating students.

Kirby got up from his stool. Alan, who had been bending over the bar, stood up straight. Kirby put both arms around him and pulled him in. He felt the boy's warm cheek against the side of his head.

"I'm glad you saw it," Alan said, his voice filling Kirby's consciousness. "There's no way I could have told you."